D1073753

Whore

by Tanika Lynch

This is a work of fiction. The authors have invented the characters. Any resemblance to actual persons, living or dead, is purely coincidental.

If you have purchased this book with a 'dull' or missing cover—You have possibly purchased an unauthorized or stolen book. Please immediately contact the publisher advising where, when and how you purchased this book.

Compilation and Introduction copyright © 2006 by Triple Crown Publications
4449 Easton Way, 2nd Floor
Columbus, Ohio 43219
www.TripleCrownPublications.com

Library of Congress Control Number: 2005910630
ISBN: 0-9767894-6-9
ISBN 13: 978-0-9767894-6-8
Cover Design/Graphics: www.MarionDesigns.com
Author: Tanika Lynch
Typesetting: Holscher Type and Design
Associate Editor: Maxine Thompson
Editor-in-Chief: Mia McPherson
Consulting: Vickie M. Stringer

Copyright © 2006 by Triple Crown Publications. All rights reserved. No part of this book may be reproduced in any form without permission from the publisher, except by reviewer who may quote brief passages to be printed in a newspaper or magazine.

First Trade Paperback Edition Printing April 2006
10 9 8 7 6 5 4 3 2 1

Printed in the United States of America

dedication

This novel is dedicated to my beautiful, intelligent daughter, Shantayvea Lonyea Edwards, Grandma Lue Nell Lynch, my sidekick, Michelle R. Leven, the family of Joshlyn L. Payne, the wonderful woman who recognized my talents, Amy Morris, C/O Mallory Wilson (R.I.P.) and to all my people, especially the ladies holding it down on lock!

Tanika Lynch

Triple Crown Publications presents . . .

Tanika Lynch

acknowledgements

Thank you God for being so good to me, and showing me favor, even as I lay in the belly of the beast. Many had no faith in me, while others totally abandoned me. But in the midst of it all, you kept me. I prayed for my season to come, and after being patient, and waiting out you, you opened the door of opportunity and blessed me with Vickie Stringer, and the Triple Crown family. You touched Vickie's heart, and put faith in her for me. Without you I'm nothing, but with you I became a published author. Thank you God for this Blessing, and bless you Vickie for making my dreams come true!

Grandma Nell, thanks for sacrificing your golden years to raise my child. You told me to put God first, and all things would be possible. Because of your constant prayers I've been changed and molded. I'm coming home an accomplished woman because of you. Shantayvea, I did this for you, baby. Let me always be a motivating force within your life, as you have been in mine.

Michelle R. Leven, My #1, what would I have done without you? You helped me through all this, and stood

Tanika Lynch

v

by my side in my darkest hours. A simple thank you is an insult. But words need not be spoken, it's written in the heart.

To my soldierettes on LOCK, who held me up, and stuck closer than blood. Suge, Nakesha, Barbara & Stephon, Bianca F., D'Andrea, Timarra (Mar-Mar), Crystal, Selena, Toria, Teshena, Dino & Lana, Yvonne J., Toya, Tonya H., Tip (Kandis), Cypress, Christina, Tamica J., Alison, Stephanie Johnson, Latosca, Coretta, Danita, Boy, Keisha & Amy, Keya, Felicia, Towanna & Regina T.

My cherished loved ones, Derrick, Eric, Brittany, Dreena, Dawayna, Lil' Wayne, Darell, Lil' D, Sherece (Ree-Ree) & Brandon Parker, Tyrone & Jennifer 'show me love at Karmonos, aunt', Desmond, Sharonda & Demetrius Lunch, Myra & Dawanye, Gyra & Frank, Allisa (Toto), Sabrina (Nikki), My dudes, Cephas Byrd, and Kenny, Chick & Boo, Chris Colt, James Eichelburger, My girls Tracy (T-Mac) McCalvin, Bebe Payne & Jennifer Ybarra. Sell my book y'all!!!

Y. Perkins, Paula Taylor, Portia Andrews, Shelton, L. Sullivan, Cynthia Tuddles, Flemings, Mrs. Lewis, O. Williams, Walton, Rhodes, (Suga) Johnson, J. Conway, Perry, Parker, J. Wade, Sgts Deshields, Majors, Davis Payne and Schloss, McDaniels, E. Chapmen, R. Watson, Dominique Richmond, C. Dudley, (P.A.W) Andrews –White, Madden, Carter, Chapell, Henry, S. Skates, Coleman, Harding, Ross, Robinson, Harwick, Karvell, both Thompsons and all the others at Scotts & H.V.C that kept me encouraged, and focused on life. Thank you.

And a special shout out to all my Detroit natives. Help a young sistah bring home the crown! And I'll

Tanika Lynch

always represent my city. Spread the word about my book Charles Pugh, Bushman and all those down at FM 98. WJLB, DJ Ray O'Shay, Frank over at City Slickers and the Broadway, Sounds of the city, all the Detroit hair & nail salons, Marvella's Bar & grill, the players, pimps and Hustlers! Help me reach the other level of the game, and get me a hook up with a movie deal. I'm tryin' to live! And to the non-believers, get on yo' job, and step up yo' game. Don't miss your blessing cuz I'm getting mine!

Tanika Lynch

Triple Crown Publications presents . . .

Tanika Lynch

prologue

As I watch my brother Paul and my sister Ivory play in the yard with no knowledge at all of how life is hard, I shed tears. I am saddened because I know when they're a little older, one day they'll have to know. Know about the pimps and pushers in the streets.

I sit back and wonder what kind of people they will attract. Will my sister meet a man who will beat her or make her do drugs and will my brother grow up to be a meaningless thug? Or will they grow up to be a lawyer, a doctor, or even a nurse? But life is not a movie, and we can not rehearse. All that I can do is tell them, pray, then hope ... that they won't see that side of life some day.

1

Triple Crown Publications presents . . .

Tanika Lynch

chapter
one

"Stay right here," Kamone said to her baby brother Paul and younger sister Ivory, who both sat on the dirty carpet in their one bedroom apartment, watching cartoons. "I'm going to make us something to eat. Don't come outta here for nothing. Ya'll hear me?"

"Um huh," Ivory answered, nodding her head as she ran her fingers through her Barbie doll's nappy, Vaseline-packed hair. "Paul said he want chicken nuggets. Didn't you, Paul?" Ivory looked over at her baby brother, who paid neither girl any attention as he concentrated on the TV screen. Although Ivory was only six, she looked out for her brother who was three years her junior.

Kamone knew Ivory was lying. "We ain't got no nuggets, lil' mama. But I'll make us somethin' hot to eat–OK?"

"Oookay," Ivory moaned in disappointment as she continued to play with her doll.

Tanika Lynch

Before Kamone could even open the door good, she could hear the moaning and grunting noises coming from the living room, where her mother lay upon a sheetless mattress, pleasuring a trick. She quickly closed the door so that Paul and Ivory couldn't hear and walked with her eyes glued to the floor as she passed the two on her way to the kitchen.

Roaches scattered amongst the piles of dirty dishes that covered the entire length of the kitchen counter. Kamone quickly washed out one of the two skillets they owned before opening the refrigerator and snatching up an open package of bologna, three slices of American cheese and an almost empty bottle of mayo. Her hands shook as she placed the skillet onto the stove and threw three slices of the bologna inside, trying her best to ignore the nasty things the trick said to her mother.

As she flipped the bologna over, slicing the sides with a fork, she couldn't help but to glance over at the pair, but quickly turned her head when she met the unnatural stare of the cockeyed, bumpy-faced, banana-complected man who was long stroking her mother.

"Give it to me, bitch!" the trick shouted, banging her mother faster as he persistently watched Kamone. "You want this dick, don't you?"

"Fuck this pussy, Daddy," her mother moaned as she whipped her long, stringy blond hair around her shoulder. "It's all yours."

Tanika Lynch

Whore

When Kamone looked again, the man was still staring, making her feel as if he wished it were her instead of her mother he was screwing. Her hands shook violently as she carelessly spread the mayo onto the six slices of molding bread. She wanted to just run and hide, but she had promised her siblings a hot meal.

She quickly placed the meat onto the bread as the trick became belligerently loud, pumping excessively. She nearly dropped the hot skillet, burning herself, as he screamed out in an explosive orgasm.

"You nasty white bitch!" he cried over and over as his body trembled and jerked.

Her mother rolled over onto her back, panting with an expressionless face, reaching her shaky hand over onto the wooden stand that sat beside the let out couch for her last Virginia Slim cigarette.

The trick stood up smiling at Kamone as nut mixed with vagina secretions dripped from his long, still erect penis onto the floor. Kamone held her breath, trying not to inhale the revolting odors of her mother's fishy vagina and the man's musty body that hung in the air. Stepping over a pile of dirty clothes and empty Colt 45 bottles, Kamone walked by, clinching the sandwiches to her chest as if the man would steal them. She nearly jumped out of her skin when he grabbed her arm.

"Suga, dis yo' daughter?" he asked, towering

5

over Kamone's small frame with a predatorial look in his eyes. On the verge of salivating, he took in her five foot, 14-year-old curvy figure.

"That's my brown suga baby," Suga replied with a smirk upon her thin lips. "But she ain't ready foe a big boy like you—is ya baby?" she said, looking into Kamone's bucked eyes as she blew smoke out of her long crooked nose.

"Let her go."

"Come on, Suga," the trick whined as veins began to pulsate in his penis. "I'll give you another blow and ten extra dollars. Just let me jack off on her thigh. I won't hurt her," he promised, licking his large ashy white lips as if he could taste her.

"I said no!" Suga yelled, raising up from her bed. "Now let her go."

The trick slowly released his grip as Kamone yanked her arm away with tears welling up in her big green eyes.

"One day I'ma have that." He grinned and began to stroke his penis with speed. "Take a good look at this dick and remember it cuz it's yours."

Kamone looked down at the man's hairless privates seeing pus-filled bumps and dried up cum upon his long saggy nutsack before she took off running into the other room, slamming the door behind her and shaking in fear.

"Sandwiches!" Ivory yelled happily, throwing her doll to the floor, with Paul hot on her trail. "Thank you, sister." She smiled and snatched two

Tanika Lynch

sandwiches into her grasp, then turned and handed one to Paul, who stood dancing around in his soiled diaper, as if the floor were hot.

"Pick ... pick the green stuff off the bread," Kamone stuttered, still in dismay.

"I like the green stuff," Ivory giggled, taking a huge bite from her sandwich as if she hadn't eaten in days.

Paul, who was a very frail child, took a seat on the floor, and took baby bites while he continued to stare blankly at the television.

Kamone took a seat next to them at a loss for words and appetite. All she could think about was that nasty man's big filthy penis, and what he would have done to her if her mother had given him permission. Kamone was 14 years old and nowhere near being a virgin. Yet none of the people she had slept with were of her own free will.

Triple Crown Publications presents . . .

Tanika Lynch

chapter
two

"Hey, babydoll," the short, dark-complected hooker named Allisa said to Kamone as she passed her on her way out the apartment building. "You got some gum in that bag? My breath smells like shit." She placed her hand up to her bright pink lips and blew into it.

"Naw, Auntie Lisa." Kamone giggled. "Mama Cookie sent me to the store to pick up a few things."

"Is yo' mama at home? I went up there but nobody answered."

"She up there," Kamone huffed, rolling her eyes into the back of her head.

"Tell that scandalous bitch I need my red heels back." Allisa twitched her lips back and forth as if feinding for a hit. "See, that's why I don't let her borrow shit. She neva' return nothin'."

"Yeah, that's mama." Kamone giggled and slowly walked off. "I'll tell her though," she said over

her shoulder as Allisa walked out.

Kamone quickly made her way up several flights of stairs beyond her own apartment, anxious to get her mouth on the fried chicken and other dishes that Cookie had made. It was sure to be a much better meal than the bologna sandwiches that she was forced to feed Ivory and Paul earlier in the day. Cookie could cook a rat and make it taste like steak.

When she opened Cookie's apartment door, the aroma of freshly made coconut cake roamed throughout the house. "Mmm uum," she said, inhaling deeply as she made her way to the kitchen where Cookie stood over the stove dressed in a huge silk black slip, run-down slippers and yellow rollers all over her head.

"You in here hookin' it up."

"I wanted to surprise you," Cookie replied as she placed several ears of corn into a large deep pot. "But I forgot that nose of yours can smell cake a mile away." She smiled. "Did you get the right brand of hot sauce? You know that that fake mess just tears my stomach right on up," she explained, lifting up her braless breasts and rubbing one of her three stomachs.

"Yeah, Mama Cookie." Kamone laughed, placing the bag onto the square-shaped table and removing a bottle of Louisiana hot sauce, a bag of plain skins and a bottle of Wild Irish Rose. "I got the fake stuff last time cuz they were outta your

Tanika Lynch

brand. But I'll neva' do that again." She frowned, then fanned her hand in front of her nose. "You had the whole building smellin' like doo-doo for a week."

"Shut yo' mouth." Cookie let out a heavy chuckle from the pit of her belly. "Pass me that bottle," she ordered, reaching out her enormous hand.

"Mama Cookie, you shouldn't be drinkin' wit' yo' bad health and all, and dem people down at the store said they can't let me get your wine no more cause the police crackin' down," Kamone warned, slowly giving Cookie the bottle of cheap wine.

"Baby," Cookie began, quickly twisting off the cap, "my bad health gots nothin' to do wit' this wine, hear? Men, good dope and crazy hoes like yo' mama liable to put me in my grave 'foe this wine do. Don't worry 'bout gettin' the wine no mo'. I'll send one them gals afta it." Cookie placed the small bottle up to her oversized lips and drank nearly half.

Kamone laughed as she watched Cookie stick out her big white tongue and wiggle it around as if the wine were hot in her mouth. "That's some good shit," Cookie said to herself as she screwed the top back on tightly and placed it beside her on the counter.

"Now, reach up yonder, and grab me some plates," she ordered, turning back around to tend to her food. "Get foe' of em'. I know that ole hillbilly bitch mammie of your'n needs somethin' on her

stomach. All that bitch do is fuck, then do a blow, fuck, then do a blow. Lord, I'll tell ya, I don't know how I put up with that skinny bitch all these years." Cookie sucked her teeth in disgust as she fixed up the plates.

"Baby, you tell Suga I said I'ma be needin' my money this week. Now, I know she been sick, but she betta' shake that shit and get out there, and make my money! If it wasn't for ya'll kids, I'da been tossed her out on her 'coney ass. She ain't no use to me no moe' anyhow in the condition she in. Pass me that foil." Cookie pointed toward the corner of the counter. "Suga done got just as ugly as the cracks of my ass." Cookie frowned, making Kamone bend over in laughter, just imagining what the insides of Cookie's big ass looked like.

"I hope I don't look like that when I get older," Kamone replied.

"Now, I know you at that age where ya smellin' ya self, and that odor of your'n gonna attract lots of men. You always been the prettiest girl I eva' seen. But because of yo' beauty, you gonna experience a lot in life, both good and bad. But whateva' you do, whatever you go through, don't you eva' be nothin' like yo' mama, hear?"

"Yes, ma'am," Kamone replied quickly. "I'll never be nothin' like her. Just as soon as I get old enough, I'ma take Paul and Ivory, and we goin' to Hollywood. I'ma be famous. I'ma be a singer like Tina Marie and Patty LaBelle."

Tanika Lynch

Whore

"That's right, baby." Cookie smiled, handing her the wrapped plates she had placed into a plastic bag. "Believe in yo' self, and don't let nobody take yo' dreams away, hear? They all you got."

"Yes, ma'am." Kamone lowered her head and thought about all the times her mother told her she'd never amount to anything.

"You wanna wait on this cornbread to get done?" Cookie asked. "It's almost there." She opened the oven and stuck a fork into the middle of the homemade bread.

"Naw," Kamone replied, picking up the paper sack filled with the goodies she had bought with Cookie's spare change, and placing it inside the plastic bag with the rest of the food. "I already been gone too long, and ain't no tellin' what done happened by now."

"Hurry along, baby." Cookie picked up her bottle of wine. "Make sho' you tell Suga what I said and bring back my dishes tomorrow. Oh, yeah, if that big nose, bald-headed bitch Norma Gene down there wit' yo' mama, tell her I said to gather the girls up and come eat."

"OK, Mama Cookie." Kamone giggled. With her bags in tow, she walked down the hall, grinning from ear to ear, thinking about the smiles on Paul and Ivory's faces when they would see all the goodies she had hustled up for them. Suga hated when she brought home food from Cookie's house, and would forbid any of her kids to ask Cookie for any-

thing, especially food. Suga hated the way Cookie talked about her in front of the other hoes, and she didn't want Cookie to think she needed her for anything, especially feeding and clothing her own kids. But there wasn't a drop of food in the house, not even bread, and Kamone wasn't about to let her siblings go to bed hungry because of her mother's pride.

When she walked into the apartment, her mother and two of her hooker friends, Norma Gene and Honey, sat on the dirty, tan-colored couch, deep in their nods. She couldn't help but to laugh, looking at the three. Norma Gene sat on one end, slouched over so badly that her head appeared to be in her lap. Suga sat in the middle, her head tilted backwards and her legs gaped wide open, exposing her hairy blond crotch. Honey sat on the other side of Suga, slob running from her open mouth and her blond wig twisted sideways.

"Norma!" Kamone yelled, scaring the woman awake. "Mama Cookie said get yo' ugly, big-nose behind up and gather up the girls to come eat."

"What?" Norma frowned, wiping slob from the corner of her mouth as she looked at Kamone through seemingly closed eyes. "Yeah, yeah, I'll do it when I get good and got damn ready to," she snapped before falling back into her nod.

Kamone stood there a moment longer, flaring up her nose in disgust at their appearances before heading to the bedroom, where Paul and Ivory

Tanika Lynch

awaited her. She slowly opened the door wanting to surprise the two, already knowing they would trample her like a stampede of elephants.

"Ivooory, Paaaul, look what ..." She stopped dead in her tracks when she opened the door completely and saw Ivory quickly placing her hands behind her back and looking as if she had swallowed a bird.

"Hi, sister," she blurted out, jumping to her feet.

"What ya'll in here doing?" Kamone wrinkled her nose suspiciously at Paul, who was still sitting on his knees, looking back at her, then at the naked doll laying in front of him with a piece of fabric wrapped around her arm.

"Nothin', sister," Ivory answered, backing away from the doll.

"Lil' mama, what you got behind your back?" Kamone placed the bag of food onto the floor as she went toward Ivory. "What you hiding?"

"Nothin'," Ivory whined.

Kamone grabbed Ivory, spun her around and almost had a stroke when she saw a bloody syringe wrapped tightly in Ivory's little hands. "Drop it," she demanded calmly, trying to make sure that Ivory didn't make any sudden movement and stick herself. Kamone could feel her heart pounding in her chest.

"I sorry, sister," she cried, her bottom lip quivering.

"I know you are," Kamone assured her. "Just

drop it."

Ivory did as she was told, then quickly ran toward Kamone and grabbed her leg, hugging it tightly. "I sorry, sister! Don't whoop the butt!" she screamed, sobbing deeply.

"How many times have I told ya'll not to play with them things?" Kamone shouted, pried Ivory off her leg and shook her by the arms. "Did you stick yourself with it? Did you stick Paul?" Frantically, she examined Ivory's arms for needle pricks, then Paul's.

"No, sister, I not play doctor on me and Paul. We just wanted to play doctor on dolly," Ivory whimpered. "Mama and her friends play doctor all the time."

Kamone looked sympathetically into Ivory's watery green eyes, realizing that her six-year-old mind didn't know any better. She was just imitating what she had seen the adults around her doing.

"Tell me the truth, lil' mama. I won't be mad. Did you play doctor on yourself and Paul?"

"No, sister. I not lie to you. We just did it to dolly," Ivory answered softly. "Can we eat now, please?" Ivory eyeballed the bag as she played with her fingers.

"Paul, did Ivory play doctor on you?" Kamone asked, looking into his eyes intensely. Paul shook his head in disagreement as his thick eyebrows came together. "I better not ever catch ya'll playing with needles again," Kamone said, looking back

Tanika Lynch

and forth at the two. "Ya'll coulda' hurt ya'll selves."

"I sorry," Ivory replied, running and hugging her leg again as Paul followed suit.

"Lil' mama, take Paul and go wash ya'll hands real good, then we can eat."

Ivory said nothing as she grabbed Paul's hand and nearly dragged him to the bathroom.

Kamone picked up the bloody syringe and the bag of food before stomping off into the living room. "Mama!" she screamed as loudly as she could, making all three women jump. "How could you be so careless to leave this needle laying where Paul and Ivory could get it? Don't you care 'bout yo' own kids, mama?"

Suga smiled as she slowly sat up removing the hair from her face. "Let 'em poke their fuckin' eyeballs out for all I care. They had no business fuckin' around in here anyways. Give me my shit." She reached out her shaky hand.

"What you mean you don't care?" Kamone shouted. "Mama, you're sick with HIV and you still livin' life like you're normal! They coulda' got infected! What if ..."

Before Kamone could finish, Suga jumped up, snatched the needle and slapped her so hard that she flew backwards into the wall. "How dare you tell my business in front of company, bitch!" Suga yelled, slobbing at the mouth like a vicious dog.

"Mmmm, I knew somethin' was wrong wit' you,

ya pale-ass bitch!" Norma Gene jumped in, as she and Honey rose to their feet and headed toward the door.

"That's why Cookie told us not to let you use our needles. I should stump yo' ass for even keepin' the shit a secret."

"Um," Honey said as she fixed her crooked wig and skirt. "And you be out there fuckin' people without protection. Ugh! I can't wait to tell everybody. Somebody gone kill yo' ass!"

"Get out!" Suga screamed. "Get the fuck outta my house!"

"We going, bitch." Norma Gene laughed on her way out the door. "We don't wanna be around yo' contagious ass anyways."

Suga turned her attention back to Kamone, who was still against the wall, holding her red, puffy cheek. "I told you not ta tell nobody!" Suga cried. "How the fuck you expect me to get out there and make money if everybody know what I got?"

Guilt slowly crept into Kamone's heart as her mind wandered back two months earlier to the afternoon when she found her mother on the living room couch, balled up crying. The positive results that Suga had received from the clinic that morning were still crumpled up in her hand. Kamone had never seen her mother so distraught. After hearing Suga out, Kamone made a vow to her mother to keep her illness a secret.

"I'm sorry, mama," Kamone cried. "I ... I was

Tanika Lynch

just worried 'bout Paul and..."

"Fuck them!" she screamed. "I don't know why the fuck I kept them anyways! I got too many mouths to feed, and now you done fucked up my hustle!" She smacked Kamone again. "And what the fuck you got in that bag, huh?" She snatched at the bag.

"It's, it's just some stuff for us to eat, mama. I brought back something for you too," she said, holding the bag tightly.

"You done been down there beggin' for food again?" Suga said through tight lips as she tried to rip open the bag.

"Mama, stop!" Kamone wailed, trying her best to protect their supper. "Paul and Ivory are hungry, mama! They ain't ate all day!"

"They'll eat when I fed 'em! Now, give me this bag, bitch!" Suga yelled as she and Kamone began tussling with the bag until it tore open, and the wrapped food and goodies fell to the floor.

Kamone lay on top of the food as her mother struggled to get it from under her with one hand, holding the bloody syringe in the other. Finally, Suga became tired and straddled over Kamone's body, as she placed the syringe up to her neck.

"You think you betta' than me, don't cha'?" Suga asked, staring hatefully into her daughter's eyes.

Kamone just looked at her mother, too scared to talk or make any kind of movement.

"You think you're prettier than me, smarter than me and I bet you think yo' pussy betta' than mine, huh?" she screamed, now biting down on her bottom lip. "How would you feel if I stuck this needle in ya, and give you what I got? I bet you wouldn't think you were betta' than me then. Face it, ladybug, we're two peas in a pod. Yo' daddy gave you a good fuckin', just like mine did me. We both dumb, poor and neither of us got nobody that loves us. You just like me, lil' bitch! The only difference is, you got niggar blood in ya. You's a ugly, black, niggar bitch, and you'll neva' amount to shit! But since you think you so grown, and you can take care of my kids betta' than me, you can have em'." Suga got up, stumbled toward the couch, grabbed her cheap black purse and placed her dirty syringe into it before putting on her fake fox coat and red heels. "I feel sorry for ya, girl," Suga mumbled as she walked toward the door. "You'll neva' know what it's like to be me until you walk a mile in my shoes."

"How do you know what it's like to walk a mile in your shoes, when you got on somebody else's?" Kamone asked calmly, watching her mother look down at Allisa's red heels.

"You always did have a sense of humor," Suga smirked. "But soon that laughter will turn to tears. You gonna cry and cry until you got no more tears left, just like me. Remember, baby, you came from me, got my blood in yo' veins and you'll neva' be shit, just like Mama." Suga threw her head back with dignity before slamming the door in her daughter's face for the last time.

Kamone sat up, looking back at the mashed food as tears began rolling rapidly down her beautiful face. She knew her mother meant what she said. She was gone for good this time. Now she was stuck with two kids ages six and two, and no way to support them. But she'd be damned if she allowed the system to tear them apart. She was all they had and they were all she had. Without each other, life just wasn't worth living.

Ivory and Paul, who had been standing in the hall peeking around the corner, ran into the living room and stood over Kamone grinning from ear to ear as if they didn't have a care in the world.

"Sister, can we eat now?" Ivory asked, eyeballing the smashed food as she sucked on her index finger. She didn't realize or care if this would be the last good meal they'd ever have.

Tanika Lynch

Triple Crown Publications presents . . .

Tanika Lynch

chapter
three

Kamone's mother, Beth, known as Suga on the streets, ran away from her home in Alabama when she was just 11 years old along with her 15-year-old sister, Judy, to escape the wrath of her drunken rednecked father, Billy.

Billy was a preacher in Alabama, and also the head dragon of the Klan back in his day. He beat and molested his daughters literally from the day they came out their mother's womb. Their mother, Sue, was a weak woman who came from a poor family, and Billy was all she had. She never questioned his authority out of fear and Billy's way was always the right way. When Beth was three years old, her mother died of a brain aneurism, but Billy lead the girls to believe that she died of a broken heart because they were such horrible kids.

After years of being tortured by their sick, twisted, preaching father, who used God to manipulate them, Judy snapped. One night after Billy had

severely raped Beth, then passed out butt-naked in a drunken slumber, Judy gathered up the few belongings that she and Beth owned. Before she left, she set fire to the small shack with Billy in it.

The girls ran as far as they could from their home, then hitchhiked a ride with a nice, old black man who was headed to Detroit to visit relatives. They told the man their story and how they had no money, and no place to go. The nice old man told them that he had a cousin in Detroit who could probably give them shelter and maybe even a job to support themselves. The girls were grateful for whatever they could get. They just didn't want to go back to Alabama, and they prayed that their father was dead.

When the old man hit the city of Detroit, it appeared to be Las Vegas to the slow-living country girls. As he walked them to the door of the apartment building, in the Downtown Detroit area, the girls held each other and giggled as if they were stepping into the White House. The place was considered a dump to the natives, but to the unsophisticated girls, it was glamorous.

They stood nervous and buckeyed as the old man introduced them to his cousin, Nate. Nate was in his early thirties, nearly 6' 4", with a slender build. His long, jet black hair was permed and slicked to the back. The girls took him to be a millionaire since he was wearing a black silk shirt, black leather pants, shiny black shoes and a ton of

Tanika Lynch

Whore

gold around his neck. He smiled down at them with dollar signs in his eyes, already knowing why his cousin, Leroy, had brought them.

"These gals from Alabama," Leroy said, with a slick smirk on his wrinkled face. "Got no place to go, and no money. I thought you'd take em' in, and help em' out a little. They ain't fresh, but they new to the city."

"Thanks, cuz." Nate smiled, flashing two golden teeth in the front of his mouth. "I'll take good care of 'em," he said, giving Leroy a wink as he allowed the girls in.

The naive girls looked back at the nice old man who had helped them, but once he turned his back to leave, he never looked back. He walked off, shaking his head in pity. Not at himself, but for the two lost souls he handed over to his cousin, who was one of the biggest pimps around. Leroy himself had retired from pimpin' long ago, but he knew good pussy when he saw it. He didn't feel bad about what he had done. He knew that if he didn't get them, someone else would. So he may as well help keep the family business going.

Within weeks, Nate turned them out to heroin, cocaine and selling their bodies from dusk 'til dawn. He named them Suga and Spice. Suga for Beth, because she was so young, innocent in appearance and very obedient; Spice for Judy, because she had fiery red hair, a rebellious nature and had to be beaten several times by Nate for hav-

ing a sharp lip.

Within a year of their arrival, Suga became pregnant with Nate's ninth child. Kamone was born on the floor of Nate's apartment, delivered by his main ho, Cookie, who would also become the caretaker of the child, while her mother was sent out to prostitute.

Kamone was born with natural beauty. Thick jet black hair, big green eyes and skin the color of smooth peanut butter. Even though born drug addicted, she was very healthy and showed no signs of being an addicted child other than spells of constant crying.

Kamone had a close relationship with her father as a baby. Nate loved her to death. Out of all his children, Kamone was the most gorgeous. He called her his million dollar baby, and already had plans for her to be a ho just as soon as she became of age. And on her fifth birthday, he decided to be the first one to break her in.

She would never forget that day. It was the beginning of a seemingly unbreakable cycle.

Cookie and a few of the other girls all chipped in and bought her a pretty pink and white cake from Baskin-Robbins. They also shoplifted a bunch of outfits and pretty panties just for her. By the end of the day her father sent most of the hookers, including her mother, back on the streets while he, Cookie and Spice sat doing lines off the marbled table in the living room.

Tanika Lynch

Whore

She was in her father's room sitting on the edge of the bed playing with her new Cabbage Patch doll and watching TV when Nate walked in, closing the door behind him as he loosened his pants.

"You Daddy's big girl now," he said, looking down at her with beet red eyes as his stiff penis dangled from his pants. "Daddy gotta put a price on you," he said, pushing her back onto the bed. "That means Daddy gotta test his product."

Kamone didn't understand what all that meant but she would never forget the pain she felt as her father entered her and covered her mouth to muffle her screams.

After he finished he carried her out to Cookie and Spice to clean her up. Spice said nothing as she bathed her bleeding niece, but Kamone would never forget the look in her aunt's eyes.

A few months later, Nate died after shooting some bad dope into his veins. When word got around that Spice had given Nate the dope, Suga and Spice took Kamone and fled before the angry mob of hoes killed them for killing their pimp.

For a while the three lived in a hotel room. Most of the time Kamone was left alone, but many times Suga brought her tricks back to the room to receive extra money. She'd make Kamone watch as she turned tricks and sometimes, Suga would allow the men to do things to Kamone depending on how bad she was fiending.

All that came to an end when Spice walked in

and caught a trick licking Kamone's vagina as Suga jacked him off. Spice stabbed the man several times as he tried to grab his clothes and run from the room naked. She then turned around and beat Suga almost beyond recognition.

Months later, they moved into a small house in the ghetto on a street called Hastings, located by the Chrysler Freeway. It was there that most of Kamone's worst nightmares were created, leaving her with haunting memories that would forever disturb her.

She cried for days after witnessing Spice delivering Suga's second child. A boy, which was born stillborn. She could still see the small black and blue baby, covered in bright red blood, and what appeared to be guts. She screamed as she watched her mother wrap the baby up in the bloody sheet he was born on and throw him into the dumpster like an old pair of shoes before walking down the alley on her way back to the stroll. But her worst memory was when she saw her Aunt Spice being murdered.

One of Spice's tricks stalked her and followed her home one night. He crawled in through the broken basement window, and caught Spice nodding on the floor in the living room. Kamone was awakened by her screams, and stood at the top of the stairs, crying, out of sight of the killer, as she watched him beat Spice with a steel pipe. He was screaming something about herpes, and giving it to

Tanika Lynch

his wife. At the time, Kamone didn't know what herpes meant, but she knew it had to be something really bad for the man to wanna hurt Spice like that.

For two days she was left in the locked house starving, with Spice's cold, bloated, bloody rotting body. She didn't understand death so she didn't comprehend that Spice was dead. She just thought she was hurt badly. Spice was Kamone's world and her protector. Spice was the only person who had shown her affection and love. She didn't know what she would do if her aunt wasn't around to look after her.

"Wake up, auntie," she pleaded as she tried her best to clean the blood off Spice's face but the more she wiped, the more blood gushed out. She tried helping her up so she could go upstairs and rest in her bed but Spice was just too heavy. Finally, Kamone got so desperate to make Spice better that she took the needle that lay beside her lifeless body and stuck it in Spice's arm like she had seen her mother do many times before, but even that didn't work. At last she just gave in and ran upstairs to get her blanket off her mattress before lying on the floor beside Spice and covering them up trying to keep her warm.

When Suga did finally come back home and found her baby covered in blood asleep next to her sister's dead body, she broke down crying. It was the first time that Kamone had ever seen her moth-

Tanika Lynch

er cry and probably the last. But instead of getting Spice some help, Suga changed Kamone into some clean clothes, packed their belongings, and stole the gold necklace from around Spice's neck before catching a bus downtown to Nate's old apartment.

With Nate being gone, Cookie became the head ho in charge and business was better than Nate could have ever ran it. Suga begged Cookie to take them back. She told her that she had killed Spice for what she had done to Nate and showed her the bloody blanket that Kamone had used to cover them up with as evidence.

Cookie really didn't believe the lie, but she quickly accepted them back for the sake of Kamone. She could tell by the dead look in the child's eyes that she had been through hell and back living on the streets with her mother.

Cookie had always loved Kamone as if she were her own and she knew a child as beautiful as Kamone would become a warped adult, living in a such an environment. Yet there was nothing she could do about it other than love and protect her as best she could.

Cookie had one of her younger girls to bathe Kamone and fix her something hot to eat before laying her to sleep in Cookie's waterbed. While Cookie washed Suga's greasy hair she slapped some cherry red lipstick onto her chapped lips and thick black eyeliner around her dull, forest green eyes before throwing her back onto the stroll with a funky ass and the same outfit she'd been wearing for a week straight.

Cookie had never cared for Suga because of the fact that Suga had done something for Nate that she had never been able to do, and that was give him a child. But she knew that Suga was an obedient ho, regardless of her greedy drug habit. Plus, the tricks loved that hillbilly bitch and she always brought in the most money. She wasn't pretty like she was when Nate first got a hold of her but she was still a young tenda', and rumor had it that she did magical tricks with her mouth that kept the tricks running back for more.

Cookie cared less who did what. All she cared about was them getting out there and making her that money. They could walk, limp or crawl their way to the stroll but no matter what, they'd better report back to her with no less than half a grand or more, every night.

Cookie was nowhere near as brutal as Nate once was and all the hoes respected her like a mother figure. That's why her business grew so rapidly. Every ho in Detroit wanted to be down with Cookie. She showed them love, gave them good advice, didn't abuse them like many others had done, and fed them home-cooked meals every day. She gave them something they never had—love. But they knew she meant business, and if they slacked up on their business, she put her foot in their asses just like a real mother would do.

Cookie now owned the run-down building, and all her girls had their own places. But every time they came and went, they had to check in with her. She had a tight system, and she made sure all her girls were alive and well.

Cookie had much experience under her belt in both hoin' and pimpin'. Her father and two of her brothers were pimps, and she was Nate's first ho. She taught him almost everything he knew, leaving him with no choice but to love her. She was loyal to the bone, and helped him to build up his establishment, making him the pimp of all pimps. She recruited runaways, fiends or homeless women. She didn't care if they were cute, ugly, short or tall, Nate needed them all. Once Nate recognized her worth, he took her off the streets and made her his house ho. She was too valuable to lose to the streets.

Cookie was in her late 30s, but she looked much older. Drugs, along with hardcore whoring took its toll on her long ago. She was fat, extra black and toothless. Her titties hung down to her belly button, but she had a good grade of hair and a pussy of platinum gold!

Her legs and arms were covered with abscesses that had the tendency to bust open, like an overcooked microwave hot dog, when they chose to. But that didn't stop her shootin' up her dope. The war scars that covered her face and various parts of her body told the tales of how many times she almost lost her life to the stroll. She may have been the ugliest woman to walk God's green earth, but she was 'bout her business and had a heart of gold toward children.

For years she made sure that Kamone was always groomed and fed. She even taught Kamone how to read and write. Cookie also became Suga's personal mid-wife over the years, delivering three more babies, which were all by tricks and born drug-addicted, except for the last.

After Kamone came Ivory. She was born two months prematurely with an extra finger on each hand. Cookie nursed the baby to health and placed strings around the extra fingers, cutting off their circulation until they turned black and fell off. Other than that, Ivory was a normal baby and just as beautiful as Kamone, but darker, almost as if she were pure black. But her curly, jet black locks and bright green eyes gave her away as being biracial.

The third child, also a girl, was born four months prematurely, with her heart on the outside of her chest. She died just hours after being delivered.

Then came Master Paul, a name given to him by Cookie. During Suga's entire pregnancy, Cookie took her off the stroll and also off drugs. She cried watching Suga kick, whine and beg for a blow but for some reason, Cookie believed that God had purpose for this child and she wanted him to be born pure. Plus, she was tired of nursing Suga's drug

Tanika Lynch

addicted babies to health.

Consequently, Paul was born weighing eight pounds, nine ounces. He was Suga's biggest baby, and for some reason, he barely cried. To the present day, he barely spoke. His father had to be of Arabic or Hispanic descent because Paul was a fuzzy baby with silky straight black hair, thick naturally arched eyebrows, dark, hazel teardrop-shaped eyes and his skin color. He was a tad bit darker than his mother yet much lighter than both his sisters.

Kamone loved her siblings and took care of them like they were her babies since the day they were born. She was determined to never allow anyone to hurt them like she had been hurt and she put that on her life!

Tanika Lynch

chapter
four

Kamone glanced over her shoulder to make sure that no one was watching as she stuffed two packages of pork chops into the ugly pea-green duffle bag she carried on her shoulder. She then scurried down several other aisles of the market throwing different items into the bag until it became bulky and almost unable to zip.

For two weeks now she had been shoplifting from this same store and never once had she been caught. She had gotten so confident in her abilities that she decided to take as much stuff as she could so she wouldn't have to come back for a while. She usually went to the checkout counter and bought a package of gum or other small items but this time her bag was too bulky to take that risk. So she headed straight to the door.

Her heart began to pound as she made her way toward the exit. She tried her best to look normal but it seemed like all eyes were on her. She quickly pushed open the big glass door and smiled as she stepped one foot out but before she knew it, a strong hand was pulling her back by the shoulder.

"Where do you think you're going, thief?" said the deep voice of a man with a strong accent.

Kamone looked over her shoulder and stared into the eyes of a tall, dark-complected Arabic man named Sam who was the stock boy in the market.

"Hi, Sam," she said, smiling weakly. "I ... I wasn't going anywhere. I was just going out to the car to get the food stamps from my mama," she lied.

"Save it." He frowned, grabbing the bag from her as he pulled her back into the store by her too little hot pink coat and escorted her to a small, dimly lit room in the back of the store.

Kamone lowered her head in shame as other store workers and customers watched, shaking their heads in pity.

When they entered the room, another Arabic man who was the manager was sitting at a long, oval-shaped table looking over several pieces of paper.

"What do we have here?" he asked in an even stronger accent, removing his reading glasses as a smirk came upon his crater-filled face.

"I saw her in Aisle Three packing cereal into this bag," he said, throwing the bag onto the table. "So I watch her and she damn near stole the whole store then tried to leave. She comes in here every day with her shifty eyes buying bubble gum. I

Tanika Lynch

knew she was stealing but today I catch her!"

Kamone stood in silence looking down at the floor as beads of sweat curled up the baby hair on her forehead.

Saul, the manager, looked Kamone up and down, putting down the papers and opening the bag. "Well." He laughed as packages of hot dogs, canned goods, tampons and other items fell onto the table. "Looks like you were stocking up for the winter. Who sent you here to take these things?"

"No one, sir. I took them for myself," Kamone answered, still looking downward.

"Why do you steal from me?" he asked, stepping toward her with his hands upon his narrow hips.

"I didn't steal from you," she replied in a defensive tone. "I stole from the store."

"This store belongs to me therefore you take my stuff," Saul explained, raising his voice up a notch. "How old are you?" He stood in her face.

Kamone remained silent, still staring at the floor. "Do you want me to call the police, boss?" Sam asked anxiously, ready to pick up the phone.

"Yeah, go ahead," Saul replied, turning his back on Kamone. "They'll find out how old she is."

"OK, OK," she pled, grabbing Saul's arm. "I'm 14, sir. I'm sorry I stole from you, but my little brother and sister are at home starving. I didn't know what else to do."

"Where are you parents? Did they send you here to steal?" he asked, turning to face her. When he looked into her eyes, his heart dropped. She was an intriguing creature, with such angelic eyes.

"My daddy's dead, and my mother left us," she said softly. "I'm taking care of them by myself."

"She's lying!" Sam screamed. "She told me that her mother was waiting in the car with food stamps. She's a con. I'm calling the cops." He grabbed the phone.

Kamone looked at Saul with fear in her eyes as tears began to fall.

"Wait!" Saul yelled, with authority in his tone. "Sam, go back to work. I can handle this alone."

"But, Papa ..."

"You heard what I said," Saul replied. "If I need you, I'll send for you. Now leave."

Sam looked at Kamone as if she were the scum of the earth before mumbling something in Arabic and slamming the door behind him.

Saul scanned Kamone, smiling slyly as he turned his attention to the table filled with stolen goods. "You don't want me to call the police because they'll lock you up and put your brother and sister in foster care, being you have no parents, correct?" he asked as he surveyed the stolen items.

"Yes ... yes, sir. I'm all they have and if we get split up, there's no telling what will happen to them. Please, please, don't call the police. I'll work for you for free for as long as you like. I can clean really good."

Saul said nothing as he picked up items off the

table looking at the prices and putting them back down. "Who are you getting these for?" he asked, holding up the box of tampons.

"Me," she answered, turning beet red in embarrassment.

"I don't believe you," he replied, walking closer to her. "Put down your pants and show me."

"But ..."

"No buts! Either you do as I say or I call the cops."

Kamone turned away shyly as she unbuttoned her brown corduroy pants and let them fall to the floor. She then pulled down her small yellow and white floral print panties, and exposed the balled up bloody tissue she had placed between her legs in the place of a pad.

Saul removed the tissue, looking at Kamone all the while as he placed it up to his nose taking a long, deep sniff. "You smell like a wild flower." He smiled, throwing the tissue to the floor. "Here's what I'll do for you." He placed his fingers under Kamone's chin, lifting her head up to look into his eyes. "You have to pay for all the things you've stolen."

"But I don't have any money," she whined.

"No, darling," he chuckled. "I don't want currency." Saul took two of his fingers and stroked them between Kamone's legs. It seemed as though the sight of her bright red blood excited him.

"Lay on the table," he ordered, unzipping his

black and white pinstriped pants and allowing them to fall around his ankles.

She slowly pushed the stolen items to the side and lay across the table looking up at the ceiling as her heart beat rapidly in her chest.

Saul hopped over to her with his dick in his hand and quickly slipped it into her. He grabbed her by the waist and moaned things in his native language as he humped her like a stray dog. "Does it hurt? Does it hurt?" he grunted through clinched teeth as he stroked hard and fast. When he saw that what he was doing had no effect on her, he quickly flipped her over in anger and ran the head of his penis deep into her anus.

"Nooo!" she screamed, trying to get away.

"Shut your face before I call the police and have them lock all you bastards away!" he threatened, pumping her behind as hard as he could. Kamone put her face into her coat to muffle her screams as Saul pulled her long curly hair and bit on her neck.

"Damn it, you black bitch," he moaned in her ear as he came inside of her rectum. He went limp on her back, panting heavily as he slowly withdrew his soft, bloody penis. Kamone lay crying into her coat as sharp pains ran throughout her body.

After Saul regained his strength, he grabbed a few paper towels that sat on top of a filing cabinet in the corner and wiped his penis off before pulling up his pants.

"Get out," he ordered as he walked back toward

Tanika Lynch

her.

"I can't," she cried, trying to lift herself up. "It hurts."

"I hurt the same way every time you dumb Negroes come into my store to steal!" he yelled. "Now, get up and take your stolen shit before I send you to jail." He walked over to the bloody tissue that he had taken from between her legs and stomped over to the table, snatching her up by the back of her coat. "Here," he said, throwing the tissue at her. "Put your shit on, take the food and go. I've been paid in full."

Kamone shook intensely as she reached down for the tissue and placed it back into her panties. She whined in pain as she reached down again and pulled her pants back up.

"You got one minute to get that shit off my table and get outta here!" he shouted.

Kamone scrambled to put the items in the bag as Saul stood by the back exit door of the office.

It took every muscle she had in her body to lift the bag and place it over her shoulder before taking her first steps toward the door, sobbing uncontrollably.

"I bet you'll think twice before you bring your black ass back in here stealing," he said as she passed him. "Oh yeah, if you think about calling the police on me, I'll be sure to tell them about those bastard babies you've been stealing for," he threatened.

Tanika Lynch

Instantly, the anger inside Kamone took over the pain, and before she knew it she hawked up as much spit as she could and spit into the man's face, then took off running through the snow. She ran and ran like she had never run before. Even when she reached the apartments she continued to run. Different hookers tried speaking to her but she heard nothing as she shot past them like a bullet.

When she reached her apartment she collapsed and fell flat on her face in anxiety. She lay there crying, replaying the event that had just taken place. She sobbed into the floor as she thought about what would have happened had Saul called the cops. That thought alone hurt more than being raped and sodomized.

She knew that she could never take a risk like that again. She would just have to find another way to feed and clothe herself and her siblings. But no matter what she had to do, she would never allow anything or anyone to take Paul and Ivory away from her. They had already been through hell in their short life span and she knew that they depended on her for everything just like she had once depended on Spice.

She had to be strong for them all or else they wouldn't make it. Whatever she had to endure to make their lives a little better would be done without question, even if it did break her in spirit.

She wiped the tears from her eyes, stood to her feet and held her head up high as she did the secret

Tanika Lynch

knock to let Ivory know that it was her at the door.

She could hear Ivory screaming cheerfully inside as if Santa Claus were at the door with tons of gifts. Ivory quickly unlocked the door, smiling wide-eyed at Kamone as Paul hopped around like a frog behind her, knowing that it was time to eat.

"Sister!" Ivory yelled as she stood in the doorway. "What kinda goodies you got us this time?"

Kamone couldn't help but smile as she looked at their innocent faces, unaware of what she had gone through just to feed them. But their smiles made her feel like what she been through was well worth it.

Even though she had no choice in the matter, she had just officially turned her first trick. But what she had experienced with Saul would be nothing compared to what was awaiting her in the near future.

Triple Crown Publications presents . . .

44

Tanika Lynch

chapter
five

Paul and Ivory sat giggling on the couch, watching in amazement as Kamone sang a tune by Anita Baker into the hairbrush, pretending it was her mic. She sang with all her might, as she fell to her knees, grabbing Ivory's hand. "Ya got ta hold on a lil' longer! Ya gotta to beee a lil' stronger!" As she continued on, she picked up Paul and spun him around. "You can win, you can win, and everything thaaang is gonna be all right."

"Sing it, sister!" Ivory screamed, jumping to her feet and doing a little jig.

When Kamone finished, Paul clapped excitedly. "Yeeea!" He giggled, kissing her on her cheek. It had been a month since Suga had abandoned her kids. Kamone worked hard on a daily basis to keep the little ones entertained.

"You sound so pretty, sister." Ivory smiled in admiration. "Are you gonna be on the radio like other people who sing?"

"One day ..." Kamone smiled, a dreamy gaze in her eyes. She placed Paul onto the floor. "One day, you, me and Paul are gonna be laid up in our big mansion, drinking Kool-Aid from crystal glasses and have five cars apiece, parked outside, right next to our big swimming pool."

"Yeah," Ivory said excitedly, as if she could see it all now. "And we gonna have all the pretty dresses, all the necklaces and all the food in the world. We can eat cheeseburgers and pizza, like rich people."

"All you think about is food." Kamone laughed.

"Yep," Ivory agreed. "And when I grow up, I'ma work at McDonald's, so I can eat all the Happy Meals I want."

"And you gonna be a big, fat, green-eyed pig," Kamone teased. "Paul, what you wanna be when you grow up?"

"Doggie," Paul answered happily, getting down on all fours and panting like a little dog as he licked the back of his hand like a cat.

"Look at Paul." Ivory pointed as she and Kamone laughed at Paul until they cried. As they continued to watch Paul make a fool of himself, someone pounded loudly at the door as if they were trying to come through it.

"That's not the secret knock," Ivory whispered. "It's a stranger, huh, sister?"

"Go in the room," Kamone whispered, hurrying the two along before going to the door. She looked

Tanika Lynch

out the peephole and saw Cookie leaning against her big wooden cane with her other hand propped on her gigantic hip and her nostrils flared out as wide as Africa.

Kamone cracked open the door just enough to see her, giving her a phony smile as she said, "Hey, Mama Cookie. What you doin' out your apartment?"

"Kamone, I know that straggly bitch-ass mammie of your'n been sendin' you down to lie for her skank ass!" Cookie yelled. "That country bumpkin' might be infected, but ain't nobody on earth been sick for a month straight! She been down here secretly turnin' tricks and spendin' my money on dope! Now, where she at? Ain't nobody seen her in a month! The bitch betta' be in here stretched out dead cuz I'ma 'bout ta kill her if she ain't!" Cookie threatened, barging her way inside. "Where ya at, bitch?" Cookie shouted, looking around the small apartment. "You can run, but cha' can't hide and where eva' ya hidden, ya betta have my money, or it's gonna be me and you, white girl! I'ma beat cha' for the old, the new and the shit you think I don't know about!" Cookie snatched open the cabinet door under the kitchen sink, knowing Suga was small enough to fit.

"Mama Cookie, listen," Kamone said, following behind the woman frantically.

"I don't wanna hear it, baby," Cookie said, making her way to the bathroom. "I love you and all,

but if Suga ain't got my cheese ya'll all the hell outta here today! I don't love nobody mo' than my money, not even myself!" she declared, busting the bathroom door open with her boxing glove-shaped hands and looking high and low.

"Mama Cookie ..."

"Move, gal," Cookie ordered, looking at the closed bedroom door and laughing to herself as she removed a switchblade from deep within her bra.

"Watch out, bitch, cuz here I come! And I'ma cut out that rottin' pussy ta make sho' you can't use it again!" she roared, dropping her cane and wobbling full speed toward the door, knocking it right off the hinges.

Paul and Ivory screamed at the top of their lungs, running far off into the corner, holding each other as they watched Cookie's angry big fat ass twirling the knife around like she was in a Bruce Lee movie.

"Mama Cookie!" Kamone screamed, angry at the woman for startling the kids. "I been tryin' to tell you, she ain't here!"

"Well lead me to her baby," she ordered, snatching her cane from Kamone. "This a life or death situation and I ain't leavin' 'til I get my dough."

"I don't know where she's at," Kamone whimpered.

"What cha' mean?" Cookie asked, looking confused.

"She left us and she ain't comin' back."

Tanika Lynch

Whore

Cookie shook her head in shame, placing the knife back into her titties.

"Well," she began, following Kamone into the living room, "how you been supportin' you and the babies?"

"I been stealin'," Kamone answered, pouting as she folded her arms and flopped onto the couch. "I didn't know what else to do. I was thinking about trying to get a job at a restaurant in Greek Town, but I don't know if they'll hire somebody my age."

"Well, where ya'll was plannin' on livin', baby? Did you think I'd never find out 'bout this?"

"I was just hoping that you'd feel sorry for us if I told you mama was real sick, and just forget about us until I came up with a way to make some money."

"Kamone, you too young to be takin' on adult responsibilities. You ain't gotta lick on education and that pretty face won't get you no job at some high classed work place."

"I'm not a kid anymore, Mama Cookie. I'm very capable of takin' care of them kids. It's just I was thinkin' maybe we could come live with you for a while." She looked at Cookie with the saddest puppy dog eyes. "I can do all the chores 'round the house, run errands and do the shoppin'. And I promise Paul and Ivory will be so good you won't even know they there."

"Baby, I'm too old to be puttin' up wit' kids again. I mean, I love ya'll, but my health gettin'

worse and I can barely get around. Besides I already got a buildin' full of hoes to manage and the thangs you offered to do, my girls handle all that.

"Kamone, babydoll, I know you might not wanna hear this, but I'ma have to call Child Protective Services to come pick ya'll up. This apartment can go to one of my newest girls–the fresh meat that keep my money flowin'. Maybe it's best the state put ya with normal people so ya'll can get some schoolin' and do thangs kids 'pose ta do."

"Mama Cookie, please!" Kamone begged, hot tears marching down her face. "Please, don't do this to us! You know how the system works. They'll split us up, and ain't no tellin' when we'll see each other again." Kamone fell to her knees, holding Cookie's leg as she begged for mercy. "I'll do anything! Just please, don't call the people!"

Cookie looked down at Kamone, crying like the day she was born, then looked over her broad shoulder at Ivory and Paul, who stood in the hall-way, crying along with their sister. Her heart went out to them and there was only one thing she could do.

"Kamone, stand up from there and be the woman you claim to be," she ordered, shaking the girl from her leg.

Kamone stood up, shaking like a cold dog with her head hung low.

Tanika Lynch

Whore

"How you spectin' to raise these kids and you lookin' like you 'bout to have a nervous break-down? Now, I done did some thankin', and I believe you old enough and strong enough to hold this household down. Gal, look at me when I'm talkin' to you.

"Stop holdin' yo' head to the ground," Cookie demanded, making Kamone give her eye contact. "I think it's time for you ta get out there and make you some money. You'll make thousands every night wit' you being so young and pretty. Men will pay just to smell yo' panties, hear?

"I don't care what goes on, or how much you make, but if you wanna get on my payroll, and live in this apartment rent free, I expect half a grand every night, and not a penny short. Now, eva' since you was a baby, I knew this day would come. Shit," she chuckled, "ya been around it all yo' life. This yo' destiny. But, I always said if you decided to hook, I'd look after ya. It's the best I have ya rather than some low-life, dirty bastard gettin' his claws into ya and beatin' you senselessly with hot coat hangers, or whateva' they do nowadays, messin' up yo' pretty face, and neva' lettin' you see a dime of yo' own money. I love you, babydoll, and I wish you and the babies didn't have to suffer like this.

"But life ain't made to be easy, and you gotta roll with the punches or get rolled ova'. I'ma give you 'til tomorrow ta think about my offer. And if you serious about this, I'll be spectin' you down at my

Tanika Lynch

apartment 'round noon so I can have one of my girls teach you the tricks of the trade, or else I'll have to contact the propa' authorities."

Cookie dug into her titties, pulling out a wad of money, and peeled Kamone a twenty off top. "This ta get you and the babies something hot ta eat tonight," Cookie said, handing it to Kamone. "You stay out them folks store foe you catch a felony and get a record, hear?" she advised, heading toward the door. "Oh, and, baby," she turned to face her, "you neva' did bring my dishes back."

Kamone looked over at Paul and Ivory, who were clueless to the seriousness at hand, before she turned to Cookie, and replied, "I'll bring them tomorrow. A ... around noon."

Cookie did her famous chuckle and swayed her head back and forth as she began talking to herself. "Good Lord, I'ma have a house full of devastated, angry hoes when they see who's new on the block.

"Ya'll gone back in that room and watch cartoons," Cookie said to Paul and Ivory as she handed them both a bag of Doritos. "I bet' not find no crumbs on my carpet, hear?" she called as they ran off. "And don't let me catch ya'll ramblin' through my shit, or jumpin' in my bed," she hollered down the hall.

"Thank you, Mama Cookie," Kamone said, smiling faintly. "I promise they'll be good."

"They betta' be. My nerves already bad. I can't take all that noise."

Tanika Lynch

Whore

"Them babies ain't gon' make no more noise than all these cackling hoes running in and out of here all day long," Brittany said as she walked into the apartment, sat on the floor and stretched her long tawny limbs across the carpet. A wildly glamorous beauty, big wigs and long ponytails constantly adorned her head. Men loved her perfectly chiseled calves and strong thighs. Brittany was what most pimps referred to as the bottom bitch of the flock. She was the head ho. Anytime something went down that Cookie couldn't handle, Brittany stepped up to the plate. Over the years she'd also captured Cookie's heart and going against Brittany meant going against Cookie.

Cookie looked Kamone up and down in an appraising manner. She took inventory of Kamone before turning to Brittany. "Make my baby a big girl, hear, Brittany? Teach her everythang you know. She's yo' special project. Don't disappoint me."

"Have I ever?" Brittany replied as she sat a large plastic case on the living room table, ready to go to work. "Honey," Brittany replied as Cookie walked off, "when I get though with you, you're gonna look like a whole new person." Brittany picked up several different containers of makeup and went to work on Kamone's face like Edward Scissorhands.

"I don't wanna look like a clown," Kamone said, sitting as still as a statue while Brittany plucked her eyebrows.

Tanika Lynch

"I'm offended," Brittany gasped, placing her hand up to her chest as if she were about to have a heart attack. "Look at my face, honey. Do I look like a damn clown to you?"

Kamone studied Brittany's dark chocolate, oval-shaped face seeing that the black blotches that stained her face had been cleverly hidden with foundation. Her eyeshadow and babydoll lashes brought attention to the gray contacts she wore in her sleepy eyes. The bright-colored lipstick she wore on her pouty lips appeared to be smooth and kissable. But her thin, drawn-on eyebrows made her seem to be in constant shock and she had a few stubbly hairs on her chin that needed plucking.

"OK," Kamone finally answered. "I trust you."

"You have no choice," Brittany replied without cracking a smile. "Cookie assigned you to me. You're my project."

Kamone sat quietly as Brittany moved on to her hair, flat-ironing her poodle curls and making it bone straight down to the small of her back.

"OK, boo-boo. Let's get dressed for our ladies' night out," Brittany said, spraying the finishing touches of oil sheen onto Kamone's already shiny hair.

Brittany lead her into a room in Cookie's apartment that all the girls referred to as the Room to Stardom. Inside, there were tons upon tons of enticing outfits, padded bras, panties, stockings and hats. There were several shoe racks of different

Tanika Lynch

sized and colored boots, heels and platform shoes. On the long cherry oak dresser lay an assortment of costume jewelry, wigs and other accessories. On the coat hooks against the wall hung a variety of fake mink, fox and leather coats. Every girl that Cookie got was groomed, then taken to this room to select their first outfit and a wig, if one was needed.

Kamone stood stuck in astonishment at all the beautiful things she never knew occupied the room as Brittany sized her up and picked out an outfit for them both.

"Come on, honey," Brittany said, handing Kamone a slinky, soft rose-colored mini-dress, a pair of matching leather ankle boots and a pearl choker.

"Let's go make this money."

Kamone looked at the enchanting outfit, and her stomach began to bubble.

"Brittany, I don't know if I'll look right in this. I never wore anything that showed my body and I ... I can't walk in heels."

"Take your clothes off," Brittany ordered.

"What?" Kamone giggled. "I'm shy."

"Honey, you's a ho now, 'kay? You can't get paid being shy. If you can't show me your body, how you expect to show a stranger?"

Kamone swallowed hard, slowly shedding her dingy threads as Brittany stood over her like a prison guard.

"Damn!" Brittany replied, staring at Kamone's body. "You sho' is hooked up to be 14, girl. You could use a lil' sun wit' cha pale ass, though, and some of that hair needs to be shaved off your muff." She pulled the curly hair on Kamone's privates. "But other than that, you flawless. Gone and get dressed before you make Ms. Brittany jealous." She playfully clawed Kamone like a cat.

Kamone giggled as she looked down at the bushel of hair that covered her vagina. No one had taught her how to groom herself. She thought a woman was supposed to look that way.

She quickly put on her outfit as Brittany got dressed behind her. "Could you help me put this on?" she asked, turning to face Brittany with the choker in her hand.

"What the ...!" Kamone shouted, stumbling backwards in shock observing Brittany's naked body.

"What's wrong with you?" Brittany laughed, tucking her long flimsy penis between her butt crack. "You act like you seen a ghost."

"Brittany ... you a boy!"

"Technically, I'ma man," she laughed. "But believe me, honey, this monkey don't stop no show. You won't believe how many so-called straight men love Ms. Brittany. Sometimes they pay me to suck my dick. Ain't that somethin'?" she replied, slipping on her black velvet super mini-dress.

Tanika Lynch

Whore

"But how you get them titties?" Kamone asked, still in shock.

"A lil' pullin' and tuggin' mixed with some hormone pills works wonders," she explained, jiggling her nice-sized breasts. "Girl, you betta' prepare yo' self cuz you're gonna see a lot of strange things. You'll meet strange people who'll ask you to do weird shit. But if that money is right, you just betta' act like it's normal, or you'll never make it out there."

"I don't know if I can do this," Kamone whimpered, looking as if she were about to cry.

"Awww, baby. You don't have to be scared," Brittany replied, running her fingers through Kamone's hair. "Kamone, nobody's forcing you to do this. You have a choice. Either go to a home, or do what you gotta do to survive until you can find a betta' way. I don't wanna see no girl your age out there in them mean streets. But sometimes, we gotta do what we gotta do. But no matter what you do, be the best at it. I'ma teach you everything I know, every trick in the book. And you betta' not tell a soul our secrets or I'll scratch ya eyeballs out," Brittany joked, making Kamone laugh. "Now, put on them heels, and let me show you how to strut that stuff."

Triple Crown Publications presents . . .

Tanika Lynch

chapter
six

Kamone zipped up her dark gray, waist-length mink coat, trying to keep warm as she stood against the wall of the Fox Theatre in Downtown Detroit. She looked around, nervously observing what seemed like a hundred prostitutes of all shapes, sizes and colors, prancing up and down Woodward Avenue chasing cars and even flashing themselves to vehicles that drove by.

Brittany roamed amongst the other hookers, yet kept a close eye on Kamone, allowing that she was afraid. Brittany also noticed the envy in the eyes of the other hoes as they checked out the sweet new meat, mad that they had some real competition now. They giggled and whispered as they passed her by, trying to make her feel uncomfortable and out of place.

In reality, Brittany knew that Kamone was out of place. She looked like a rose blooming amongst dandelions. Jealousy stopped others from giving

her credit, but she was without a doubt the most gorgeous girl on the stroll. Yet, she just didn't have the confidence she needed to back it up. Brittany wanted to run to her rescue, but she knew that Kamone had to learn on her own, just like she had, because she wouldn't always be around to have her back.

Before long, a dirty, beat up red station wagon pulled up to the curb in front of Kamone. The passenger's side window rolled down, and out popped the head of a seemingly young white man, wearing a red bandanna, dark tinted glasses and sporting a clean shave. "Hey, babe, need a ride?" he asked.

Kamone looked around as if he were talking to someone else before replying.

"Yeah, you." He smiled at Kamone. "Come on, babe. I don't have all night." Kamone took a deep breath as she looked around and spotted Brittany watching before taking baby steps to the car, trying her best not to tip over her five-inch-heeled boots.

When she opened the passenger's door, she noticed that the fairly attractive man only had one leg. The other was cut off at the knee.

"That's–that's OK," she stuttered. "I don't need a ride."

"What's the matter, babe?" the man asked, sounding disappointed. "I'm not a cop." He went into his pocket and pulled out a fist full of bills. "I got lots of money and I'll pay whatever you want.

Tanika Lynch

You're one smokin' mama."

"I ... I gotta go." Kamone panicked, slamming the door and almost slipped on an ice patch as she ran to find Brittany.

Before the door could even slam good another older, less attractive hooker ran up to the car, bending over in his face to expose her saggy, meat-less-looking breasts. "Ya dating tonight, Daddy?" She flashed a smile.

"Um ... yeah," he answered, trying to look around her for Kamone. "But I only got ten dol-lars," he lied, quickly putting his money away.

"But I just seen ..."

"I said I only got ten dollars," he repeated with an attitude.

The woman rolled her eyes and twisted her lips but wasted no time jumping into the car.

"Brittany! Brittany!" Kamone bellowed, running through the crowd of laughing whores. "Brittany, I couldn't do it!" she cried, throwing herself into Brittany's arms. "He had one leg and ..."

Before Kamone knew it, Brittany pushed her away and slapped her across the face. "Gain your composure!" she demanded. "Look at these ugly bitches making fun of you," she replied, looking around at the giggling women. "Neva' let em' see you sweat, Kamone."

"That puppy ain't ready ta hang wit' the big dogs," an oversized hooker named Tater remarked as she walked by. "Put that bitch back on the

porch."

"Dis shit out here is for real women, baby girl," Bop added, walking next to Tater. "Yo, Britt, you want us to bring some milk and cookies back?"

Tater bent over in laughter. "What about a towel so you can wipe that water from behind her ears?"

"Shut yo' pig-lady lookin' ass up!" Brittany yelled, turning to face the women. "Don't make me take off these heels and stomp you like the man I really am!" she threatened in her real manly voice. Tater and all the others quickly shut up and went about their way, knowing that Brittany was capable of whooping them all single-handedly.

"Brittany, I can't do it. I ... I'm scared," Kamone admitted.

Brittany looked at Kamone's baby face, watching her shiny lips quiver. Finally, she spoke up. "Girl, if you can't show Cookie you 'bout it, you may as well kiss them kids goodbye. I told you beforehand what to expect out here. You can't concern yo' self with how a person looks.

"If that nigga's money is long enough, you shouldn't give a fuck if he wanted to fuck you wit' that stubbed leg. Look, I can't hold yo' hand through this. You need to decide what you wanna do."

"I gotta do it. I have no choice," she replied. "But would you just ... just help me," she said in frustration.

Brittany sighed, shaking her head in disappointment at the thought of what she was about to do. "I'ma help you the best way I can, all right? But remember I'm doing this because I really do care about you, and I know you really love those babies. Now, remember you asked me to help you. What happens after I help you is on you."

She grabbed Kamone's hand and led her into a vacant building. She dug into her purse and pulled out a small red pill and a tiny bottle of gin. "Open your mouth," she ordered as she twisted off the top to the liquor bottle.

"Brittany, I never drank or did drugs before," Kamone said softly.

"Look, honey, either you want me to help you or you don't. Now open your mouth."

Kamone hesitatingly opened her mouth and closed her eyes as Brittany placed the pill on her tongue then poured the gin down her throat. "What is that?" Kamone frowned, coughing and patting her burning chest.

"The pill is called Spanish fly. And you just had your first taste of gin. Baby, when that shit hit you you're gonna be so hot and horny you'll fuck a three- eyed troll." Brittany laughed. "But to make it all kick in faster," she said as she went under her wig and removed a small bag filled with a white powder substance, "I'ma give you a little bit of this."

"Naw, Brittany. I don't wanna be a fiend like my mama," Kamone said, stepping back away

from the bag.

"Girl, yo' mama was a weak bitch and a blow head," Brittany replied. "This here is white girl cocaine. You can't develop a habit from taking it one time, unless you choose to. This shit will have you feeling so good and carefree, baby. I wouldn't give you nothing to hurt you, Kamone."

"I'm just trying to help. Don't you trust me? I ain't lead you astray so far," Brittany said as she took out a book of matches and tore off the lid to put some of the cocaine on. "I do it all the time and you see I'm still a diva." She placed the lid of cocaine up to her nose holding down one nostril and inhaling deeply with the other until every last drop disappeared. "See." She smiled, rubbing her numb nose. "It's easy." She poured more onto the lid and held it out to Kamone. "Come on, honey, trust me."

Kamone took a deep breath as she carefully took the lid from Brittany and closed her eyes as she imitated what she had just seen Brittany doing. As soon as the powder went up her nose, she felt a strange tingling, then a numbness. "I can't feel my nose!" She panicked and rubbed her burning nose rapidly. "And it's in my throat!" she whined.

"Good, that means it's working." Brittany laughed. "Here." She gave Kamone the bottle of gin. "Finish this off. And in a second, you gonna feel like the most ravishing girl in the world. Now

Tanika Lynch

remember everything I taught you," Brittany said as Kamone stood up, feeling a little funny. "When you get into a car with a trick and you get bad vibes, follow your first mind and get out. I don't want you gettin' hurt out here. If you think he might be a cop tell him to pull his dick out. If he don't jump out that mutha fucka you goin' to jail. Blow jobs are one-hundred and fifty dollars and over. Don't let em' talk you down."

As Brittany reminded Kamone of the rules, Kamone stared at her vacantly as if she weren't even there. She could feel tingling sensations all throughout her body. She felt as if she were being tickled from head to toe, her vagina jumped as if it had its own heart beat and her nipples arose and stuck out like two thumbs in her skimpy dress. She flipped her long hair over to one shoulder and licked her bronze-colored lips as her eyes contracted into a sexy cat-like slant.

Brittany stopped talking and smiled to herself as she witnessed Kamone transforming before her eyes. "Ooow, bitch," she giggled. "You ready to conquer the world now, ain't you?"

"What?" Kamone giggled, tossing her hair back flirtatiously and softly biting the corner of her bottom lip.

"Yeah, baaaby, you feelin' yo' self." Brittany laughed. "Let's get back to work before I mess around and get my wee-wee hard," she joked. "I see it already. You 'bout ta clean house."

Kamone remained mute as she strutted back toward the stroll as if she had been born with a pair of heels on. She unzipped her coat and allowed it to fall off her shoulders, slightly showing off her revealing dress. The painfully ice cold wind now felt like light breeze upon her skin. She smiled carefree, floating on cloud nine as she sashayed past the other hookers with her head held high. She stood on the corner posed up like a centerfold model and within seconds a nice, expensive-looking truck pulled along side her. Kamone didn't even look back for Bittany once as she hopped inside the truck without a second question.

By the end of the night, Kamone turned more tricks than most hookers did in three days. With her good looks and slammin' young body she was in high demand. The cocaine, pills and alcohol gave her the boost of confidence and courage she needed to alter her innocent personality and turn into the sex goddess she needed to be in order to make her money in the streets.

She made Cookie's quota of five hundred dollars in less than an hour. The drugs made her so hot and horny that she would have stayed on the streets all night turning tricks, had Brittany not pulled her off the streets and taken her home.

She had never felt so beautiful, so important and so invincible in her life. She knew now that with the fast, easy money that she made on the

Tanika Lynch

stroll she would be able to give Paul, Ivory and herself a much better life than the one they had been living ... just as long as she had the drugs she needed to turn her into a sex goddess every night.

Triple Crown Publications presents . . .

Tanika Lynch

chapter
seven

"Girl, I got this one old man that pays me one hundred dollars every time he picks me up, just to piss on him," a short, high-yellow completed prostitute named Vanilla said to Kamone and two other hookers who stood on the corner in front of a liquor store on John R. Road.

"Baby, that ain't nothing," her friend Thunda laughed. "I got one that likes me to make him get butt-naked, put a dog collar around his neck, then he shits on his floor and I rub his face in it and call him a bad dog. For some reason that's the only way he can cum."

"I have one that likes me to wear his sister's high heels and step on his nuts," Kamone joined in with a laugh.

"Ugh," another hooker named Peaches said, gagging at the thought of such things. "That's some nasty shit and ya'll some nasty hoes for even doing it."

69

"We some paid hoes, too," Vanilla replied. "And that's why you been on the stroll for six years and still ain't made over a thousand dollars," she joked.

As Vanilla and Peaches got into a heated argument, Thunda noticed a patrol car approaching from a distance. "Five-O, girls," she yelled. "Get on ya'll P's and Q's."

Kamone watched as the women began stuffing drug pipes and other small objects into the cracks of their behinds, wigs and vaginas. Since she had been on the street she had never once experienced a police encounter but she heard enough about it to know what she was supposed to do. She quickly turned her back and removed the package of cocaine that Brittany had given her earlier from the top of her thigh-highs and tossed it to the ground before walking away, hoping nobody had noticed.

"Oh, Lord," Vanilla whispered, as the patrol car zoomed up onto the curb. "It's that nasty bastard, DDD, and his flunkey-ass sidekick."

Before Kamone could ask any questions, a short, chubby, young white boy jumped out and stared them down grimly as he stood against the hood of the vehicle. The driver, who was a tall, muscular, young-looking black man, got out the car, smiling handsomely as he made his way toward the women.

"All right you loose bitches!" he shouted. "Ya'll know what time it is."

Kamone looked around dumbfoundedly, listen-

Tanika Lynch

ing to the women grunt and mumble obscenities as they turned around and spread their legs and arms against the liquor store wall, before she quickly caught on and did the same.

"Well, well," he said, walking up behind Vanilla. "I see yo' low-lifed-ass pimp finally scraped up enough change to bail you out the county, huh?" he remarked, taking his foot and kicking her legs apart farther.

"I ain't got no pimp, Officer Valentine. And furthermore, why every time you see me, you make it yo' business to harass me? I'ma file a civil complaint on yo' ass. You ain't slick. You love touchin' my sexy-ass body," she said in a sassy tone.

"Bitch, I'm checkin' for dope." He laughed, pinching her nipples so hard that she cried out in agony. "You better be glad I don't embarrass you and have you bend over and cough. A tow truck with three missin' people liable to fall outta that big mutha fucka."

"You should know." Vanilla frowned and rubbed her aching nipples as he moved on to Peaches.

"What's this?" he asked, pulling a small mirror out of Peaches' jacket pocket. "I bet you do yo' lines off this, huh?"

"I use it to look at my pussy," Peaches answered sarcastically, wiggling her long tongue at him.

Officer Valentine placed the mirror under Peaches' short skirt and replied, "Shut up lying

before I put you and yo' pussy under arrest for being so ugly." Then he placed the mirror into his back pocket.

"Oh, I know you got some dope on you," he said, patting Thunda down.

"Nigga, you ain't even part of the narcotics division," Thunda commented. "You ain't even part of vice squad. You and that rookie-ass white boy just some dirty mutha fuckas!"

"I'm the police, bitch!" Officer Valentine yelled, pushing Thunda's face into the wall. "I ain't gotta be on no squad. We our own squad." He grabbed the woman by her neck and turned her around to face his partner. "Hey, Victor, you need a good ass lickin' today, son?"

"Naw," he declined. "My ass still tickles from the one she gave us last week."

"Get yo' ass off this corner," he frowned, shoving Thunda off before kicking her in the back. "You won't be makin' no money today, wit' yo' sharp talkin' ass. Talkin' 'bout some squad. Spell it!"

Kamone's heart thumped in her chest as he stood behind her, preparing to shake her down.

"This yours?" he asked, yanking Kamone's hair.

"Yes, sir," she answered quickly, refusing to get flip-lipped and have him embarrass her.

"Yes, sir?" he repeated in surprise, as he searched her. "I can't believe it, a ho with manners," he joked. "You new 'round here, ain't you?" he asked, rubbing his hands across her breasts more than once.

"A new what?" she asked, playing dumb. "I was on my way inside the store before you pulled over," she lied.

"What's your name?" he asked, running his hands down her smooth, curvaceous legs.

"Vanessa."

"I see these hoes done already taught you how to lie," he said as he stood back up. "Turn around and let me see yo' face," he ordered. Kamone followed his order, looking him dead square in the eyes. "Damn, Ma," he smiled. "You too pretty to be out here sellin' ass, don't you think?" he remarked, staring into her piercing green eyes. "What they call you, Vanessa Willams or Sparkle?" he joked. "Have you ever seen this movie, Sparkle?" he questioned, obviously admiring her as he looked her up and down.

"Yeah," she replied, turning her head away. "She was a singer."

"Did you see how her sista died?" he asked, lowering his defense. "Don't let that happen to you, Ma. You too beautiful for that."

"Why don't you gone somewhere wit' yo' nasty ass," Vanilla replied. "Girl, he ain't doin' shit but tryin' to get in yo' panties. Don't fall for his shit. That nigga a monster."

"One more word from you, and I'm takin' you in and bookin' you!" Officer Valentine threatened, shutting Vanilla up with the quickness. "How old are you?" he asked, turning his attention back to Kamone.

"22," she lied, casting her eyes downward.

"22, huh?" He smiled, flashing his perfect teeth and a set of dimples. "Who you work for?"

"Nobody," she replied, looking up at him. "Anything I do I do for myself."

"I don't buy that and I don't believe you're 22. Nor do I believe that your name is Vanessa," he replied. "I hope you know that I got mad street resources and I can find out anything I wanna know about anybody I wanna know about."

"Why would you wanna know about me?" she asked.

"Because," he said, hunching his shoulders. "Believe me, we'll see each other again and when we do I hope you'll have changed yo' career. A young pretty thang like you might get messed up in these streets. We'll have to see what we can do about that."

He took every inch of Kamone in once more before looking over at Vanilla and Peaches.

"Stay away from these flea bag bitches," he said as he turned to leave. "You might fuck around and catch somethin'."

"Ole punk ass nigga," Vanilla mumbled, dogging him and his partner as they got in their patrol car.

"Man what's up with that?" Officer Victor asked, looking curiously at his partner as they

Tanika Lynch

drove away.

"What's up with what?" Officer Valentine smiled.

"You know, the red bone," he replied. "I ain't neva' seen you be so concerned about a prostitute."

"She reminds me of somebody," he answered as he turned the corner. "She has a familiar spirit."

"Oh my God," Kamone said, grabbing her beating chest. "That cop was crazy," she said, walking over to Vanilla.

"Sho' is," Vanilla agreed, going into her purse and pulling out her lipstick. "And it looks like he got the hots for you, and that ain't a good thang. DDD is sick wit' his shit," she explained, reapplying her lipstick.

"What?" Kamone laughed. "Why do you call him DDD?"

"It's short for Dirty Dick David. David Valentine Jr. He's a young, spoiled punk who sticks his dick in everything warm. And he thinks he owns Motown. His daddy is some big-shot attorney who used to have a office in the Penobscot Building, and his twin brother a dope dealer. David is a straight up psycho. I'm tellin' you now, girl, if you see that nigga comin' you betta run."

"He can't be all that bad." Kamone laughed, under the impression that Vanilla just didn't like him.

"Let me tell you something, honey. About a year back it was this cute lil' Spanish chick that this nigga named Butchy was pimpin'. Dirty Dick David was obsessed with that girl and she wouldn't give him the time of day because Butchy woulda killed her if he found out she had any dealin' with the police.

"Next thang you know the chick was found dead, shot point blank in the head in an alley. The last time anybody seen her was in the back of David's patrol car. He arrested her after seeing her get into a car with a trick. He loves chicks that look like you. But if you love life you'll stay away from that deranged nigga. He's a strange one."

"Girl, please," Kamone scoffed and flicked her wrist in dismissal. "I'm out here to get money. I ain't foolin' 'round with no police. But he was cute though." She smiled. All of a sudden it hit her that she forgot all about her package of drugs she had thrown down. She slowly walked back over to the spot where she had dropped it trying to appear normal as she searched around for the pack, but it was no where in sight. She knew Vanilla couldn't have gotten it–she had been talking to her. Then, she realized that Thunda was gone. "Damn!" she shouted, placing her hands up to her head.

"What's the matter, girl?" Vanilla asked as she flashed her breasts to a passing by vehicle.

"Oh, nothing. I just lost my earring," she said, unwilling to share the fact that she had become addicted to drugs with Vanilla or anyone else for that matter.

Tanika Lynch

Whore

"Where you going?" Vanilla asked as she watched Kamone walking swiftly down the street.

Kamone paid no attention to her question as she broke into a light jog. She had to find Brittany and get some more drugs. There was no way possible that she could turn a trick with those disgusting men without doing a hit first. She was lost without cocaine and even though she wouldn't admit it, she had become a coke whore.

She didn't know just how much she really depended on the drugs and she never would have imagined the extent she would go to just to get it. Even though she was still young and beautiful she was on her way to becoming a junkie and doing things only junkies did, just like her mother!

Tanika Lynch

Triple Crown Publications presents . . .

Tanika Lynch

chapter
eight

"Brittany!" Kamone yelled as she burst into Cookie's apartment. "Brittany! she yelled again, looking around like a lost child.

"I'm in here," Brittany shouted out down the hall from Cookie's room.

Kamone took off down the hall, bursting into the room panting and sweating like a wild animal in heat.

"Sister!" Ivory screamed excitedly, waving her hands happily as she and Paul sat beside Cookie eating pigs' feet. Kamone paid Ivory no attention as she looked down at Brittany wide-eyed.

"Brittany, I need to see you."

"What's wrong with you?" Brittany questioned, looking curiously at Kamone as she sat on the edge of the bed rubbing her long, swollen, ugly feet.

"You done robbed somebody, gal?" Cookie asked, sopping her pigs' feet in hot sauce.

"Naw, Mama Cookie. I just really need to talk with Brittany," she replied, staring Brittany down.

"I done taught Master Paul hows to hold his ding-ding over the toilet. It was 'bout time this boy got outta diapers being he gone be three tomorrow. You ain't forgot 'bout Master's birthday, have ya, Kamone?" Cookie asked, gnawing on the plump pigs' feet.

"Um ..." Kamone said, glancing at Paul, who smiled cheerfully with a greasy mouth. "Naw, I didn't forget. I'ma 'bout to go pick him up some stuff right after I talk to Brittany," she lied, giving Brittany the eye as she nodded her head toward the hall.

Brittany tightened the blue silk scarf she wore around her head as she got up and followed Kamone into the hall, closing the door behind her.

"Brittany, I need some more 'caine," Kamone whispered, moving her legs around as if she had to urgently use the bathroom. "The police came searchin' us, and I had to throw it. I think Thunda ganked me for it cuz ..."

"Ugh," Brittany interrupted, looking Kamone up and down. "Honey you just done got pitiful. You need to slow your roll. Us divas don't allow drugs to control us, we control the drugs, remember? You startin' to use it for personal reasons. You don't need it every time you turn a trick,

Tanika Lynch

Kamone. And I can't keep supplying your habit. That shit is costly. I told you from the gettie up that what happened after I give it to you the first time was on you. Now I been nice feeding you every time you come to me for it, but now I feel like you playin' on me."

"No, I'm not!" Kamone yelled. "I need it! I'll pay you whatever you want for it, I got money! Just give it to me!" she demanded, looking Brittany all around wondering where she had it hidden on her body.

"Girl ..." Brittany frowned, grabbing Kamone's arm and pulling her away from Cookie's bedroom door. "Stop talkin' all loud. What you tryin' to do, get me murdered? If Cookie find out I got you using, she'll kill me dead."

"Fuck Cookie," Kamone whispered in an angry tone, stomping her feet. "I'll go in there and tell her myself if you don't give me none."

Brittany twisted her neck, crossed her arms, stepped one foot forward and flared up her nose. "Oh, we playin' cutthroat now?" she asked, smirking all the while.

"Naw, you playin' cutthroat," Kamone snapped. "You just mad because you know when I'm on 'caine, I turn more tricks then yo' faggot ass can turn in a lifetime."

Brittany's mouth flew open as she grabbed at her chest and stared at Kamone in shock. "Is that so? Well, dig this. How about you take yo' extra

fine, superstar ass down in the hood and buy it yourself? How 'bout that?"

"I got long loot," Kamone frowned. "I don't care 'bout buying my own shit. Yeah, tell me where to go. That way I don't need you. I'll know where to get it myself."

"Um huh," Brittany chuckled. "Well, go on down there on Mack Road, to the Bewick market. There's a lot of young kats down there, but I want you to look for this lil' Latina chick named Michelle. Tell her Ms. Brittany sent you, or else she won't deal with you."

"Is that all?" Kamone laughed. "You act like I was going to gang territory. I done been on Mack before."

"Since I did you a favor," Brittany said, going into her bra and pulling out two crisp one hundred dollar bills, "do me a favor and give her this. Tell her I said hook me up with a number two, and make it good."

"What's a number two?"

"She know what it is," Brittany said, smiling wickedly. "And don't worry about getting Paul's stuff for his little party. I'll take care of that."

"Thanks." Kamone smiled, taking off toward the door. "I'll be back in a jiffy."

"Yeah," Brittany said to herself as she headed back to the room. "That's what you think. You gone learn 'bout callin' Ms. Brittany a faggot."

Tanika Lynch

Whore

* * *

Kamone sat in the back of the taxi twirling the ends on her hair around her finger, checking out the scenery as she anxiously awaited reaching her destination.

It had only been a little over month and a half since Kamone took her first hit and already her addiction was full-blown. She had three hundred dollars in her purse and she planned to buy herself enough coke to last her a few days. She didn't like the thought of running back and forth to the spot like the low-lifed junkies she despised so much when she was growing up. She wasn't worried about the amount of money she was spending; she had no doubt that she would be able to make it right back no sooner than she got back on the stroll. She realized that she didn't need any pills to get her juices flowing. The cocaine did that and also made her feel so powerful over men which was the real reason she needed it so badly.

When the taxi pulled into the parking lot of the Bewick market, Kamone's stomach began to flutter knowing that she was just moments away from getting her hands on the drugs she had come to love. She was amazed at how much activity took place outside. It seemed like there was more selling going on in the parking lot than in the market itself.

"Stay right here," she said to the driver as she

placed twenty dollars into the deposit slot. "I'll be right back."

"Nooo," the old man replied, shaking his head as he turned around to get his money out the slot. "I'm from 'round here. I knows what goes on at this market. You ain't gettin' back in my cab with nothin' illegal. Get back the best way you can."

"Whatever." Kamone frowned, jumping out the cab. She ran her fingers through her hair and tugged at the bottom of her short red dress as she looked around the parking lot for the Latina girl who Brittany told her about, but from the looks of things, all boys occupied the territory.

She slowly walked up to a group of young, thuggish-looking men who stood around in a circle free-styling rap lyrics. "Excuse me," she interrupted, grabbing everyone's attention. "Do any of you know where I can find a Mexican girl named Michelle?"

"Who lookin' for her?" a neatly dressed Latino boy asked as he readjusted the baby blue skull cap he wore low to his eyes.

"Um ... it's, it's kinda personal," she replied, too ashamed to ask for drugs in front of the fine young men.

"You a fiend, baby?" a chubby boy questioned, rubbing his hairy chin as he checked her out. "I'll hook you up somethin' tight for a head job," he offered.

"Please," she frowned, throwing her hair back.

Tanika Lynch

"Do I look like a fiend? Ms. Brittany sent me down here for her."

"Oh, you know my nigga Brittany?" the Latino boy questioned, stepping forward. "I'm Michelle."

"I'm looking for a girl?" Kamone replied, studying the boy carefully and noticing how much he resembled Paul.

"She lifted up her Nike Air shirt and flashed Kamone a tittie as the group of boys bent over in laughter. "I said, I'm Michelle. Now, what's crackin'?"

Kamone turned red in embarrassment as she took Michelle out of earshot before pulling out her money, along with Brittany's. "Brittany sent me down here to get her three hundred in coke, and she gave me this two hundred for something called a number two. She said make it good."

"Make it good, huh?" Michelle smirked, taking the money into her hand, and placing it in her sock. "Damn," she said, shaking her head as if in disbelief. "She sent you to pick up a number two?"

"Yeah. Could you like hurry it up? I got business to take care of."

Michelle shot Kamone a snooty look before replying. "You um ... we gotta go pick up that number two, baby. It's back at the spot, but it's not too far from here."

"Damn," Kamone said in anger. "Well, I'll just

tell her you out. Can I get that coke though?"

"You might as well roll back to the spot wit' us. We gotta reload anyways. We don't carry that much shit on the street, shorty."

"Who is we? They gotta go, too?" Kamone asked, looking back at the men who were looking right back at her.

"Them my people," Michelle said. "We roll thick like that. When I move they move, baby."

Kamone's first mind told her to forget about the whole deal, and just come out the closet and go to someone else who could maybe help her out, but the junkie inside of her made her impatient and told her that it was a possibility that no one could help her, and she need coke right now. She knew that without it, she couldn't hit the stroll, therefore she couldn't make her money.

"They harmless, baby," Michelle assured her, sensing her dismay. "Brittany wouldn't have sent you down here if she didn't know I'd take care of you. It's rare for Brittany to send someone down here for a number two. Ya'll must be on real good terms. Besides, I already got the money, and I don't give refunds."

"Is the spot far from here?"

"Chill, baby," Michelle replied, seeing sweat rolling from her forehead as she became noticeably jittery. "I'ma hook you up swell," Michelle said, as she turned around and walked over to her boys. "Stay right here."

Tanika Lynch

Whore

Kamone became frustrated as Michelle talked to her buddies. She began to wish she hadn't insulted Brittany, that way, she could've talked her outta some dope, and she wouldn't be going through all this right now.

"Come on," Michelle said, leading Kamone to a black Malibu that was parked in the far end of the parking lot. "You can sit up front with me." She smiled, giving Kamone a flirtatious wink as she jumped into the driver's seat, and three of the seven young men she was with hopped into the back. Kamone sighed as she got into the passenger's seat and turned her head toward the window to avoid communication with Michelle and her crew, as they cruised through the ghettoed streets of Eastside Detroit.

The unexpected quietness made Kamone more uncomfortable being in a car full of strangers—hoodlums at that. She became even more skittish when they pulled up in front of a house on French Road that appeared to be vacant, but was very much alive on the outside with close to a dozen young men standing on the porch and grassless lawn.

"Come on," Michelle said, jumping out the car as her friends did the same.

"Can't I sit here?" she asked, feeling intimidated by the men who glared at her like a hungry pack of wolves.

"Awww, Shorty," Michelle replied, giving her

a friendly smile. "I know you ain't scared. I'm sure by now you use to being stared at. Ain't nobody gonna do nothin' to you while you're with me. And it's gonna take a minute for me to get Brittany's hook up together anyways."

"I'll just wait in the car," Kamone replied, feeling uncomfortable being around so many men.

"Dig. Come on in and I'll throw you a pack for being so patient," Michelle said, seeing the delight in Kamone's eyes.

"Um ... do–do you think I can go somewhere private and do it?" she whispered. "I don't like everybody knowing my business."

"No problem." Michelle smiled, walking around to the passenger's side and opening the door for her. "I promise it won't take no longer than 'bout ten minutes, then you can be on your way." She took Kamone's hand and helped her out the car.

No sooner than her feet hit the ground, the men on the porch began hooting and hollering at her as if she were a star.

Kamone held her head down and walked closely beside Michelle as she followed her into the house. She was nervous, and a little frightened by all the men, but secretly she enjoyed the attention and even giggled flirtatiously as one boy tried to lift her dress as she passed.

"This me, babyboy," Michelle said, wrapping her arm around Kamone. "So ya'll can stay out

Tanika Lynch

Whore

here while me and my girl handle our business." She smiled, throwing up a coded signal with her free hand before opening the ragged screen door for Kamone.

Inside, the place looked just as abandoned as it seemed, with only a small, black couch in the living room, accompanied by a three-inch color television that had a wire coat hanger in the back, substituting the antenna, sitting on a stack of milk crates. The carpetless living room floor was covered with potato chip bags, beer bottles and fast food wrappers as the smell of freshly-smoked marijuana reeked throughout the house.

"Here," Michelle said, going into her jeans pocket and handing Kamone a nice-sized dime package of cocaine. "Go to the bathroom and handle yo' business. By the time you come out everything should be ready. Walk straight down the hall, to the first door on the left."

"Thanks." Kamone smiled, taking off through the living room. "I'll be right out." She quickly turned the tarnished brass knob, opening the door to the dirty, empty bathroom. She paid no attention to the broken toilet that was almost filled to capacity with urine and feces, which gave the bathroom a very foul odor, as she dug into her purse for her foundation compact and a small red straw. She flipped it open and poured the bag of cocaine onto the mirror. Her nose began to run with anticipation as she placed the

straw up to it and sucked the cocaine up like a vacuum cleaner.

She stumbled back onto the door, closed her eyes and smiled as the feeling of undefeatable power began surging throughout her body. She licked her lips and rubbed her hands across her body as she enjoyed the feeling. Her hips began to sway as she looked down at herself, knowing she looked oh so sexy in her extra-short, red suede dress that fit her like a second skin with her matching thigh high boots. She felt as though she could control the universe with her sex appeal now, and even the thought of turning a few tricks with some of the dope boys outside crossed her mind. But their money had to be right before they laid hands on a sensuous young diva like herself.

Kamone looked into her compact mirror to make sure her fire engine red lipstick was still on and shook out her hair a little to give it a wild look before she stepped out the bathroom to show the dope boys the sex kitten she really was.

When she opened the door she was startled to find Michelle standing behind two of the young men who had been out on the porch. "You ready to find out what a number two is?" Michelle asked, smiling all the while.

Before Kamone could say a word or make a move, one of the men hit her dead in the face with a pair of brass knuckles, knocking her off her feet and onto her back. The blow had such an

Tanika Lynch

effect that she felt herself fading into uncon-
sciousness. The last thing she could remember
was someone grabbing her ankles and the painful
feeling of her head bumping up and down as she
was carelessly dragged down a flight of stairs
before she fell into total darkness.

Triple Crown Publications presents . . .

92

Tanika Lynch

chapter
nine

"I think the bitch tryin' to wake up," Kamone heard a man's voice faintly say as she slowly began opening her eyes. She tried to focus but her vision was a blur. She could clearly hear the voices of many people around her and she could feel the body heat of someone laying on top of her, as they thrust in and out of her vagina.

For a moment she thought she was dreaming. She tried to move but she couldn't. She tried to talk but nothing came out. She shook her pounding head trying to clear her impaired vision and when she opened her eyes again the first thing she saw was the crispy black penis of the man on top of her as he aimed it at her face and shot cum on her lips and nose area.

"Damn baby," a heavy set man said, stepping toward her as he pulled down his jogging pants. "I'm glad you decided to wake up. For a minute I thought I was about to fuck a corpse."

Tanika Lynch

Kamone began to panic as she looked around in terror at the group of men who stood around watching and laughing as they waited for their turn. Instantly she tried to get loose but her arms and legs were tightly bound with ropes and wrapped around several poles. She lay butt-naked, spread eagle on the cold pavement floor and they had gagged her mouth with something that was stuffed so far down it almost touched her tonsils and sealed it with duck tape.

"Damn you wild," the chubby man commented, as she struggled wildly to get free.

"Hurry up, nigga," a boy nicknamed Stank yelled. "Stop tryin' to make love to that street walkin' bitch like she yo' woman, dog."

The man grunted as he plunged himself inside of her paying no attention to the comments of the others. When he felt himself about to ejaculate, he pulled himself out and shot his cum upon her breasts.

"Damn, dog," Stank laughed, stepping up for his turn. "Why you nut on them pretty-ass titties? I planned on suckin' em'." Stank, who got his nickname because of the foul stench that came from his butthole, got on his knees and lifted Kamone's tied legs up as far as he could get them then rammed his long, skinny penis into her asshole. Stank yelled weird obscenities as he banged her as hard as he could, having flashbacks of what other men had done to him during several of his prison bids.

Tanika Lynch

Whore

Kamone tried to scream but it seemed like the more she tried to struggle the more aroused the man became. By the time the last of the 15 men got finished with her she lay stiff, looking lifeless. Tears rolled down her eyes constantly, but she showed no emotion. Her pain had become rage, and all she could think about was what she would do to Brittany if she made it through this.

"Damn, this the finest bitch Brittany eva' sent to us," one of the dope boys said before kicking her in the side and running off upstairs with the rest of his homies.

Kamone lay limp on the basement floor, feeling cold, in pain and wet from the cum the men left all over her beaten body. She didn't know where she was, how long she had been there or what they planned on doing with her but her main concern was what would happen to Ivory and Paul if they decided to kill her.

For nearly an hour, she lay there thinking about how she had avoided Ivory in Cookie's room, and how she had been so wrapped up in getting drugs that she had totally forgotten about Paul's third birthday. As far as she knew, she had probably missed his party. And she could only imagine the saddened looks and the thoughts that ran through Paul and Ivory's heads when she didn't show up. She realized that cocaine had taken control of her life and made her lose focus. It had become more important than the two people that she loved more

than anything. She felt as if she had to use it in order to even get the nerves to get out there, and do what had to be done. But along the way, she had lost herself.

She made a promise to herself that if she made it out of this alive, she would change her life and never use drugs again. But she still would do whatever she had to in order to keep her siblings with her. She couldn't imagine them being somewhere without her around to protect them from the cruel world that she already knew so well.

Her chain of thoughts was broken when she heard footsteps creeping down the stairs. She closed her eyes tight and began to pray to a God she knew very little about.

"Damn," Michelle chuckled, walking over to Kamone and standing over her sperm-filled body. "I see my dogz put a hurtin' on that sexy ass. They even left you tokens of appreciation, huh? Well," she began, kneeling down next to Kamone as she removed a syringe from her pocket, "I feel you deserve to know what the deal is. You see, I been doing business wit' Brittany for a minute now and I realized that the bitch is good people as long as you on her good side. To make a long story short, the nigga don't like to be crossed, disrespected or feel like she got competition.

"And you had to do one of those three thangs for her to send you down here to us. She pays me and my wreckin' crew swell to knock a bitch who thinks she's betta' than her down a few notches. As you can see, my niggaz know how to make a fine bitch feel like cat shit. Now my job is to lower yo' high class standards and turn you into a junkie in the worst way."

When Kamone heard the word "junkie" her eyes popped open in utter fear. At the very sight of the needle she began struggling to break loose. She knew all too well the effect that this particular drug had on a person and she always vowed to never become like her mother. But from all she had endured earlier, her body was weak and lacked wind.

"You might fight me right now," Michelle said as she gripped Kamone's arm and placed a piece of rubber tightly around it to get her veins good and swollen, "but by the time I let you loose, you'll be beggin' to lick my ass for another hit."

Michelle plunged the needle into Kamone's throbbing vein, and instantly the drugs took effect. Everything around Kamone became blurry as her head bobbed back and forth. Her world began to spin and she tried fighting the feeling that the drugs had on her but it was no use.

Michelle stood over her grinning as she watched Kamone's eyes rolling back into her head as her jaws clinched tightly around the dirty sock in her mouth. She knew heroin was the worst dope that the white man could have ever put on the streets. And in less than a few days, Kamone's body would

Tanika Lynch

be craving that shit.

As Michelle watched her, she realized that the girl began urinating on herself and her body was going into convulsions as she choked on the vomit that was sealed in her throat by the sock and duct tape.

"Damn!" she said, running over to remove the gag from Kamone's mouth. "I ain't tryin' ta kill you. I didn't get paid for all that." She untied her hands and lifted her up so that vomit could escape but Kamone still flopped around as if she were having a seizure. "Hey!" she screamed. "I need some help down here! I think I overdosed this bitch!"

Several of the boys came running to Michelle's call, looking on in shock as Kamone's body shook violently before going totally limp.

"You done killed the bitch!" Stank shouted. "I'm gettin' the fuck outta here before boss man came through. He gone fuck us all up if he find out 'bout this shit!"

"I ain't goin' down alone, nigga!" Michelle said, quickly untying Kamone's feet. "We all in this shit together, got paid together and we gettin' rid of her together!"

"My mama gone kill me," a chubby boy named Fat Cat whined. "I ain't neva' did no shit like this before. What we gone do wit' her, Michelle? I ain't made for prison."

"Help me pick her up," Michelle commanded, grabbing Kamone's hands.

Tanika Lynch

Whore

"It's dark outside. We can carry her out, put her in my trunk and dump this bitch in an alley somewhere."

"But she got our DNA all over her," a handsome young man named Eric said as he helped carry her out.

"Ya'll shoulda thought 'bout all that while ya'll was bangin' the bitch wit' ya'll dirty asses. That's why I don't fuck wit' men," Michelle commented in anger. "Ya'll just betta hope that the rats eat this ho before somebody finds her. I don't give a fuck. I just want her up outta here before boss man come through."

Triple Crown Publications presents . . .

Tanika Lynch

chapter
ten

Lucci rolled down the window of his money-green Impala and flicked out his cigarette butt as his partner, J-Smooth, continued to stare out the window of the parked car at the house four houses down, periodically taking a drink from the rum bottle he held between his legs.

They just came from a nightclub on the Detroit's West side, where J-Smooth ran into one of his old running buddies, who informed him that a man named Kenny was back in town, and could be found on the East side at an after-hours joint. Kenny owed Lucci and J-Smooth a large sum of money, so the two men wasted no time leaving the club and hitting the freeway, headed to the location where Kenny was last spotted.

"Man," J-Smooth said to his partner as he turned up his liquor bottle. "I'm ready to roll up in this mutha fucka, and drag that nigga out! I!m tellin' you, Lucci, I ain't 'bout to play with dude. As soon

as I see him, I'm blastin' him on the spot."

"Chill," Lucci chuckled, lighting up another square. "He gotta come out sooner or later. He can't be up in there forever. Trust me, I want his ass just as bad as you. Ain't no nigga gonna pull a nick slick-ass gank move on me, and live to tell the story. Hold up." Lucci sat up in his seat as he observed two men exiting the house. "I think it's him."

J-Smooth gulped down the rest of the liquor as he reached into the backseat for his pistol-gripped pump. "That's that loud suit wearing faggot-ass nigga!" he declared through tight lips, reaching for the door handle and dropping the liquor bottle as he jumped out.

Kenny and his friend were headed toward Kenny's truck when they heard the sound of glass shattering on the concrete close by. Kenny looked around and saw two armed men running full speed toward him in the darkness. He was such a scandalous man that he didn't even have to see the faces of the two people to know that they were after him. He took off running, leaving his friend behind as he hurdled over fences and ran into a dimly lit alley, with Lucci and J-Smooth hot on his trail.

"I'ma torture this nigga!" Lucci yelled, snagging his expensive suit pants as he jumped over a fence. "I just bought this fuckin' suit!"

The two tried keep up with the man as he bobbed and weaved his way through the alley, but Kenny was hauling ass, running for dear life. J-

Tanika Lynch

Whore

Smooth stopped in his tracks and shot at him twice, but Kenny made a sharp left turn, allowing a brick wall to take the bullets for him as he disappeared.

"Don't let him get away!" Lucci panted, running to where he'd seen him last. "Damn!" He stomped his feet in his gator boots and looked around at the many directions in which the man could have escaped. "Search that way, I'll look in the alleys," Lucci ordered, running down a narrow alley occupied by many dumpsters.

He walked swiftly down the alleyway, looking all around for any sign of Kenny. He began to search the dumpsters, thinking of where he might hide if someone were looking for him. As he was doing so, he heard a noise coming from inside of one close by. He cocked his Beretta, and stood in silence to see if he'd hear it again. When he heard the low grunts of what sounded like a wounded animal, he lowered his weapon and exhaled, thinking that it was just an alley cat trapped in the trash. When he turned to walk away, he heard it again, but this time the low grunt sounded like the word "help."

He raised his pistol again and hesitatingly walked toward the sound. He shuffled back and forth on his feet biting on his bottom lip, not knowing what to expect. He took a breath and quickly flipped back the lid aiming his gun inside. His eyes bucked in shock as he looked down at the badly beaten naked body of a light-complected female with long black hair covering her face. "What the

103

fuck?" he said almost in a whisper as he took full observation of the female. He nuzzled the head of his gun against her arm to make sure she was the one making the noise and he wasn't looking at a dead body. He slightly jumped back in surprise when she made a louder grunt.

He wiped his mouth and looked around before staring down at her once more. His street instinct kicked in telling him to just leave the situation alone and get the hell on before he got blamed, but his heart wouldn't allow his feet to move. He may have been an outlawed street thug, but he was the type of man who loved women even when they showed no love for themselves.

"J!" he shouted loudly for his partner, still staring at the girl. "J! Where you at?"

J-Smooth, who was not far away, heard his partner's call and took off running in the direction of his voice, thinking that Kenny had been found. "What's up dog?" he asked curiously, gripping his pistol's trigger tightly.

Lucci waved for him to come closer keeping his eyes glued on the girl.

"Ha ha," J-Smooth laughed as he ran closer to Lucci. "You smoked his ass, didn't you?" he questioned. His facial expression changed when he noticed the blank expression on Lucci's face before following his eyes into the dumpster.

"What's up, dog? You know this bitch or somethin'?"

Tanika Lynch

"Naw I – I heard noises coming from the dumpster and when I opened it I found her here."

"Maaan, that's why you was callin' me like a maniac? Cuz of some scum bucket ho who probably deserves to be in the trash? Dog, we been waitin' to catch up wit' Kenny punk ass for over a year and you gonna put it off for this shit? That nigga hit us for half a million. Can this bitch produce our cheese?"

"Man, would you want two motha' fucka' to find yo' mama or hot-ass lil' sister fucked up somewhere, and not help them?" he asked, looking up at his partner for the first time.

"My moms ain't got shit to do with this," J-Smooth said, getting defensive. "And if a nigga was chasin' down his chedda' in the process of finding them, I'd just have to unda' stand."

"You a sick nigga, you know that?" Lucci replied, taking off his suit jacket. "Just help me get her out."

"And you's a soft nigga," J-Smooth replied, moving away from the dumpster. "And I ain't touchin' that broad. She got noodles, doo-doo and all kinds of shit on her. I can smell the ho from here."

Lucci shook his head in disgrace of his partner before turning his attention back to Kamone and throwing his jacket over her body and carefully lifting her up.

Kamone let out soft whimpers, as if the slightest touch would kill her, as Lucci cradled her motion-

Tanika Lynch

less body in his arms, carrying her back in the direction of his car.

As he carried her, the wind blew in her thick hair carrying it away from her face. Lucci looked at Kamone, as his partner trailed behind speaking harshly on the entire situation, but Lucci didn't care. Even though her eyes were swollen shut and black, he looked past her bruises and saw just how beautiful of a girl she really was. And even though she appeared older body-wise, he could also tell that she was still very young.

He began to wonder what kind of lifestyle the girl was living that led her to this tragedy, or more importantly, what kind of animal would do something so hideous to the young girl? Maybe he was soft like his partner had mentioned but for some odd reason, he felt sorry for her and each second he held her in his arms, he grew a little more attached to her.

Regardless of whether or not she had done some dirty deeds to make whoever leave her for dead, it wasn't his concern. He wanted to know more about the girl. Who she was, and what she was in to. He felt as if fate had allowed him to be the one to find her, and he knew at that very moment that he wouldn't leave her side until he found out everything he wanted to know.

Tanika Lynch

chapter eleven

Kamone could hear the deep voice of a man as she awakened from a deep sleep. She opened her hurting eyes as far as she could and looked around the unfamiliar room. To her left she saw a seemingly tall, dark-complected man leaning back in a cushioned chair, asleep, with a black mink coat covering him. She whipped her head around toward the voices and saw another dark-complected man standing with his back to her talking to a short, white man dressed in a long white overcoat.

She automatically began flashing back to the episode she remembered last. The faces of all the different men who raped her flashed before her eyes. She sat up in a panic and screamed bloody murder, scrambling to get out of the bed.

"What the fuck?" J-Smooth yelled, startled out of his sleep. He jumped to his feet and looked around frantically as he reached for his pistol.

Lucci and the doctor quickly turned around

and struggled to keep Kamone in the bed as she ripped the IV from her arm, thinking it was a some kind of device to hold her down.

"We're not the ones who hurt you," Lucci explained, calmly restraining Kamone's arm as she kicked and punched at them wildly.

"Please, don't hurt me no more! I'm sorry! I'm sorry! I promise I won't tell nobody! Just let me go! Don't kill me!" she pleaded through her cries.

J-Smooth shook his head as he sat back down, listening to her and imagining what she had been through before they found her.

"No one is going to kill you, ma'am," the doctor explained. "You're in Receiving Hospital. These two men brought you here. They saved you. You're OK now. You're safe."

Kamone stopped fighting as she looked at Lucci, who was still holding her arms, then at J-Smooth who sat with his hand cupping his mouth and chin watching her. Kamone closed her eyes tightly and began to cry as they slowly released her.

"Ma'am," the doctor began, "you're a victim of a severe sexual assault. It seems as though you were drugged, raped and beaten. We found numerous sperm samples in and on your body. I know this might be hard for you, but do you recall what exactly happened? Do you have any idea who the assailants were that assaulted you?"

Kamone remained silent, sobbing as she

Tanika Lynch

replayed what she did remember of the incident in her head.

The doctor gave Lucci a genuine look of deep concern before continuing on. "We ran several tests on you to determine whether you contracted any STDs, and luckily you're negative of all forms. But it's too soon to determine whether you're with child or been infected with the HIV virus. I also found a large amount of narcotics in your system—heroin and cocaine. Do you recall being given those drugs or did you willingly take them yourself?"

Kamone swallowed hard and wiped her tears as she sat up again. "I don't need your help. I gotta get home now," she replied softly, trying once more to get out of the bed.

"Wow," the doctor said, grabbing her arm to stop her. "I just can't allow you to leave without informing the authorities first. A police report has to be filed and …"

"Police!" Kamone panicked. "I can't talk to the police! Nothing happened to me! I did this to myself!"

"That's scientifically impossible," the doctor said in astonishment. "Who are you trying to protect? Do you know the people who did this to you?"

"Look ain't shit to talk about. Give me my clothes and let me the fuck up outta here," she demanded.

"You don't have any clothes, ma'am," the doctor replied. "As I said, these two men claim to have found you in a trashcan completely nude. I understand you're afraid, but - "

"I said there's nothing to report!" she screamed, making the doctor jump back in surprise.

"Um ... Let me talk to her." Lucci placed his hand firmly on the doctor's shoulder. "And please don't call the police until after we talk," he asked nicely as the doctor grabbed his clipboard from the edge of the bed and walked toward the door.

"OK, but whether she wants to talk or not I still have to do my part," he informed them before exiting the room, closing the door behind him.

Lucci exhaled, looking at Kamone as she sat with her feet dangling from the other side with her arms folded, looking down at the floor. "Who did this to you?" he asked, gently taking a seat on the other side of her bed. Kamone ignored his question and continued to stare at the floor.

"Dig, I ain't the police, babygirl. You can kick it with me. I just wanna help you, that's all. I don't know you, but I think it's fucked up what happened to you. Me and my boy been down here with you all night trying to make sure you was OK."

"Dog, evidently the bitch out there bad. You see she don't give a fuck. She just another junkie bitch. Let's roll up outta here and let these muthafuckas deal with this shit." J-Smooth frowned at

Kamone as he stood up to put on his coat.

"You don't know me!" Kamone yelled defensively at him. "I ain't no junkie! If you see a junkie slap a junkie bitch!"

"Chill out," Lucci interrupted, putting his hand up and stopping J-Smooth from commenting back.

"And why you actin' like you care so much?" she asked, turning to face Lucci. "Ain't nobody eva' gave a damn about me! Not even my own mama and daddy! I ..."

Kamone stopped in mid-sentence as she studied Lucci's face. She had seen those dark brown eyes before and that smooth dark skin and those pretty lips and dimples. Then it hit her. "Ain't you that cop who called me Sparkle over there on John R?" she questioned.

"John R!" J-Smooth repeated. "I knew it! You sell pussy don't you?"

"Hold up dog," Lucci said to his partner, throwing his hand up again and turning back to Kamone. "My name is Lucci. I think you're mistaking me for my twin brother, David. Believe me, we're like night and day. But I'll admit, you do resemble Sparkle to me, too," he joked, trying to brighten her mood a little. "Since I told you my name can't you at least tell me yours? I think I deserve that much."

Kamone huffed and rolled her eyes. Finally, she replied, "Kamone. Now can you help me get outta here? I gotta get home."

"Why should I help you do that? You actin' like you wanted or somethin'. Why you don't wanna talk with the police? You didn't do nothing wrong. You're the victim."

Kamone huffed even louder, smacking her lips as she looked away from him. "I ain't yo' enemy, Kamone. A nigga like me call myself doin' a good deed. If you want us to help you, you gotta put me up on what the deal is. Me and my partner could be out and about stackin' our loot, instead of sitting here foolin' around with you.

"And you sittin' here talkin' to me like a piece of shit. All I'm askin' you to do is talk to me. Maybe I can help you."

"You can't help me. Can't nobody help me," she mumbled, sounding all choked up.

Lucci chuckled before replying. "Babygirl, evidently you don't know who you're talkin' to. I'm the man on the streets. I got people in high places that can pull all kinda strings. I don't even know you but for some reason I wanna help you. I understand you've been fucked over in life. Who haven't? But everybody's not out to harm you. It's a reason you don't want the police involved. And if you don't start talkin' soon that doctor is gonna call them."

"All right," Kamone snapped, massaging her pounding temples. She remained silent for a second, as a single tear rolled from her stinging eyes onto her face. "I'm scared they'll take me away," she answered softly.

"Take you for what?" he asked, leaning in closer to her.

"Away from my brother and sister. My mama left us, and I been taking care of them on my own. I don't wanna be on the stroll, but Mama Cookie told me I had to, or she would call Child Protective Services to pick us up."

"What the fuck is a Mama Cookie?" J-Smooth asked.

"She a madam. She took over my daddy's business after my aunt killed him for molesting me. My brother and sister are with her right now and don't even know how long I've been gone. If I don't get back soon she'll think I left them, and she'll send them to a home," she sobbed. "I only use cocaine to help me deal with the tricks. This faggot bitch Brittany set me up and sent me to a dope house where these dudes raped me and some Mexican bitch injected me with heroin while I was tied up trying to turn me into a junkie. I don't know what happened after that."

"So you tellin' me that your father molested you, and your aunt killed him? And your mother abandoned you so some bitch named Cookie put you on the stroll and that's how you're taking care of your brother and sister. Then some faggot set you up and had you raped, and drugged?" Lucci looked confused as if she had made up her story.

Kamone shook her head in agreement, as tears

rolled like water down her face.

"How old are you?" Lucci asked.

"I just turned 15."

"Maaan, is you makin' this shit up to make a nigga feel sorry foe yo' ass or what? I know how shit goes in the D, but I ain't neva' heard no shit like this," J-Smooth commented.

"Why the fuck would I lie?" Kamone yelled. "Look, I told you what you wanted to know and you don't believe me. I'm gettin' outta here. I don't need ya'll help," she declared as she jumped out the bed barefooted, dressed in a backless hospital gown.

Lucci jumped up, looking over at J-Smooth, who hunched his shoulders and threw his hands up, as if he didn't know what to do. "Kamone," Lucci called out, walking up behind her. "We'll take you back to where you need to go. I wouldn't want nothing else to happen to you."

J-Smooth rolled his head around as if in disagreement, yet he followed behind the two as they walked out the door.

"Excuse me," the doctor said, walking swiftly behind them as they headed toward the door. "You can't take this young lady. I've already informed the police, and they're on the way."

"Didn't I tell you not to call 'em?" Lucci frowned, turning to face the doctor. "Now see, I hate when muthafuckas disobey." Lucci whipped his handgun out of his waist, and hit the short doc-

Tanika Lynch

tor twice in the front of his balding head with the butt of the gun. He lifted Kamone off her feet as the doctor fell to the floor in pain, holding his head, as blood gushed from the opened gash. Nurses and other hospital staff screamed and took cover as the trio ran for the door.

"Dog, we gonna fuck around and catch a case fuckin' wit' this East side broad," J-Smooth laughed as they ran to the Impala, jumped in and burned rubber as they fled the scene.

"Awww, J," Lucci laughed, looking out his rearview mirror as he hit the busy street. "I did that for you. You been wanting excitement all night. Now, you got some."

Kamone stared out the window in a zombie-like state as Lucci drove down Chene Street, headed toward the downtown area. She thought about a hundred things at once not knowing where to start after all this.

She knew that the first thing she would do was get a hold of Ivory and Paul, wrap her arms around them and never let go. She knew that they had to be scared right now. She had never been apart from them more than a few hours. As for Cookie, there was no telling what she was thinking. But right now, Kamone could honestly give less than a fuck what she thought. She had been so naive to everything going on around her, but this brutal experience had been more than enough to open her eyes and harden her heart.

She realized that Cookie's fat ass didn't have to put her on the stroll. She had just used her situation as an excuse to recruit her into her stable in order to take her mother's place and make more money. It wouldn't have hurt her deep pockets one bit to take Kamone and the kids in. She was just a greedy, money hungry bitch who played psychological games with people's feelings. All she did every day was sit on her dimpled wide ass shooting dope, drinking and eating while she collected thousands of dollars. Kamone thought about how when she was little, she had seen Cookie stashing her money under a loosened floor board in her room. There was no telling how much money was hidden there by now.

She then drifted to Brittany's scandalous ass. At first she thought the sissy was helping her out. But now she felt as if she meant to turn her out. Then to top it off, she set her up to be raped and introduced her to heroin.

True, she had gotten high off the drugs, but when she saw Michelle's concern about her dying, she exaggerated the scene some in hopes of getting free.

She knew she had to get out. She couldn't imagine hitting the stroll and having sex with men after being raped so many times. She didn't want to use drugs ever again and if she didn't leave, things would only get worse for her. She might not be as lucky next time. She couldn't put herself, let alone

Tanika Lynch

Paul and Ivory, through that. Something had to change.

"What's on yo' mind?" Lucci asked, breaking her train of thought as he glanced over at her while lighting himself a cigarette at the red light. Kamone looked over at him with an indescribable look in her eyes and just stared.

"Well," he began, slightly smiling with the cigarette dangling from the side of his mouth, looking back and forth between Kamone and road. "Spit it out."

"I need a gun," she said plainly.

Lucci whipped around with wrinkles in his forehead as he removed the cigarette from his mouth. "You plannin' on killin' somebody or somethin'?" he questioned.

"Not really," she replied, turning her head toward the window. "I just need one for protection."

Lucci looked back at the road ahead, debating on whether giving her a gun was the right thing to do. He knew that she had been through a lot and he figured she had to be in an unstable state of mind. But then again, she was already in the streets playing dangerously and she did need something to defend herself with just in case she got herself into another situation. What made him make his decision was when he pulled up in front of the apartment building she lived in. It reminded him of a place on "A Nightmare On Elm Street."

Yet, he said nothing about the place she called home, refusing to add embarrassment upon the already humiliating ordeal.

He dug into his waist and handed her his Beretta. "Where you gonna put it?" he asked, examining her thin hospital gown. "Here," he said, taking off his dark brown, three-quarter length mink coat. "Put this on, and put it in the pocket. You can't get out the car like that."

Kamone looked at him with grateful eyes as she took the coat and put it on, placing the pistol into her coat. "I ... I know I been a real bitch to ya'll, but I just wanna thank ya'll for everything. It's just ... I never met anybody who wanted to help me without wanting something back."

"Don't mention it, babygirl," he said, hearing the hurt in her voice as she spoke. He leaned over and opened up his glove compartment for an ink pen, and grabbed Kamone's hand. "Listen, if you ever need anything, call this number," he suggested, writing down his number on the back of her hand. "Don't be scared to use it. It's still good people in the world. People think it's men like me and J that corrupt the world, but we ain't the real bad guys. We just tryin' to make a livin'."

"Speak for yo' self, you vigilante," J-Smooth replied from the backseat, as he sat with his head tilted back, and one hand covering his closed, sleepy eyes. "I'm the baddest nigga you'll eva meet."

Tanika Lynch

Whore

"Anyways," Lucci smirked, turning back to Kamone. "I hope everything works out for you, babygirl. You too young to be livin' like you livin'."

"Don't worry," she replied softly as she reached for the door handle, looking over her shoulder at him before she stepped out. "I don't plan on living like this another day." She closed the door before Lucci could respond, turning around once more to wave goodbye before disappearing into the shack.

Lucci watched her, sadly remembering the pain and hurt he'd seen in her eyes. He wanted so badly to stop her from going in and just take her to a place where she would be safe and able to heal. But he could sense that she was on some kinda mission and she wouldn't leave without her brother and sister, anyways. He could tell by her eagerness to get to them that she loved them to death and she was probably the only mother they ever knew. Yet he looked forward to hearing from her again. His heart went out to her and he was already more than willing to help her and those kids out. Her situation just tugged at his heart like that.

"Man," J-Smooth mumbled as Lucci pulled off, "I swear to God, son, I ain't neva' goin' dubbin' wit' yo' ass again, dog."

Kamone held onto the tan-colored, scum-covered wall with her other hand rested on her turning stomach as she took small steps through the

Tanika Lynch

seemingly deserted hallways headed to Cookie's apartment.

She prayed that she didn't bump into anyone along the way. She knew that the jealous whores would love to see her down and it would be the talk of the stroll for years to come. But more importantly, they might mess up her plans. With that in mind, she sped up her pace, disregarding the pain that ran all through her bones.

When she made it to Cookie's front door, she could smell the stench of chitlins boiling inside. She stood up straight, inhaled deeply and exhaled slowly as she quietly opened the door, not knowing what to expect.

When she walked in, Cookie was standing over a large steaming metal pot with a long wooden spoon in one hand and a bottle of wine in another.

"Mama Cookie," she called out almost in a whisper, hesitantly walking toward the kitchen.

Cookie turned her head toward Kamone's voice and flared up her flat large nose at the sight of her. "Um," she huffed, frowning up her lips. "I see you finally decided to leave the dopehouse and come home. I already got the low down on you ya dumb worthless bitch."

"Huh?" Kamone replied bewildered . "Mama Cookie I was raped and ..."

"Shut yo' mouth," Cookie ordered, grabbing her cane that lay propped against the stove and wobbling her way toward Kamone. "Brittany told me all about you shootin' and tootin'. Don't you stand in my face tellin' lies! You been out there gettin' high and trickin' in some dopehouse, ya mutt bitch!"

"But Mama Cookie, I swear, Brittany set me up! She had some people to beat me up and rape me. They even shot me up with ..."

Before Kamone could finish, Cookie raised up her swollen hand and back-slapped Kamone to the floor. "Don't you stand here lyin' on my Brittany!" she shouted. "Brittany wouldn't do no sucha' thang. You's a junkie, and junkies don't do shit but lie!"

"Look at me!" Kamone yelled back, pointing to her eyes. "I just got out the hospital!"

"Yeah, you probably got yo' ass kicked for stealin' that expensive coat you wearin'," Cookie replied. "You think I'm stupid? I made every game and invented all lies! Don't you eva' build up the nerves to stand in my face and lie. If it wasn't for Brittany, them bastards of your'n would be in a fosta' home eatin' oatmeal right now. Like she say it ain't they fault you turned out to be just like Suga. But let me explain this one thang." She slapped her hand onto her wide hip as she stood over Kamone. "You been gone for damn near two days and if you don't have all my money made up in twenty-four hours, I'm washin' my hands of all this shit! I'm doin' you a favor and you call yo self playin' on me."

"But, Cookie, I swear I ain't lyin'!" Kamone screamed, lying propped on one elbow as she held her throbbing jaw. "I'm tired of this shit! I don't have to lie. Who the fuck is you? I ain't goin' back out there! Didn't you hear what I said? I got raped!"

"Are you sassin' me?" Cookie snarled. "Don't no ho of mine sass me! I brought you into this world and I'll take you out with the very same hands!" she declared as she raised her abscess-infected foot and brought it down with a thump on Kamone's pelvic bone. She continuously kicked her as Kamone rolled onto her stomach howling out in pain, inching her way into the living room.

Ivory, who was awakened by all the commotion, came walking down the hallway dressed in her long pink sleep shirt, rubbing her eyes as she held her Barbie doll by the hair. Her half closed eyes popped wide open when she saw Cookie huddling over Kamone, attacking her like an angry grizzly bear. Ivory squawked loudly as she charged toward Cookie full speed.

"Leave sister alone!" she demanded, kicking Cookie's ankles and hitting her on the butt with her doll's body. "Get off her!"

"Get yo' ass back in that room!" Cookie shouted, turning around and slapping her clear across the room.

When Kamone heard Ivory crying she flipped onto her back and looked around the room. Her

Tanika Lynch

blood instantly began to boil when she saw Ivory lying on the kitchen floor with blood running from her busted lip. Right then it was on!

She quickly reached into the pocket of her coat and pulled out the gun, closing her eyes tightly as she aimed and squeezed the trigger twice. Everything seemed to go in slow motion as Kamone opened her eyes to find Cookie still standing over her with a flabbergasted expression as she looked down at the crimson red blood that stained the middle of her mint green-colored silk gown.

"You ... you shot me," Cookie stuttered in disbelief as she touched her stomach and stared at the blood in disbelief. "Babygirl, you shot yo' mama!"

"You ain't my mama, you sloppy bitch!" Kamone declared through clenched teeth as she jumped to her feet. "And don't no bitch, not even my mama, put they hands on my sister!" She pulled the trigger twice more.

Cookie's mouth dropped open as the bullets ripped through her flesh. She looked like Fred Sanford as she dropped her cane, grabbed her bloody chest and staggered backwards. As she did so, she tripped over Ivory and stumbled into the stove. Kamone ran over and snatched Ivory off the floor as the back of Cookie's gown caught fire from the gas stove, and the brewing pot of chitlins fell to the floor, splashing all over Cookie's feet and legs. Cookie screamed out like a banshee as she stumbled all over the kitchen, catching fire to sev-

eral flammable objects.

Kamone dragged Ivory into Cookie's room, seeing that Paul still lay sleeping peacefully, undisturbed by the confusion. "Lil' mama, get Paul," Kamone ordered, as she ran over to the spot where she witnessed Cookie hiding money. When she pulled back the floor board, she found nothing. "Damn it!" she screamed, looking around the room. From where she stood, she could see the flames blazing and spreading into the living room area. She knew she had to get them out before they became trapped, but she was determined to find all that money. She wasn't leaving empty-handed.

She ran over to Cookie's dresser, snatching out every drawer and emptying its contents onto the floor. Her heart dropped when she pulled out Cookie's underwear drawer, and two large, rubber-banded stacks of money fell to her feet. She picked up the money and placed it into her coat along with the gun before double-checking for more. She knew there had to be more—much more!

"I'm scared," Ivory whined, holding Paul's hand as he stood half awake watching her rummaging through Cookie's bloomers.

She knew she couldn't waste another second trying to be greedy. Smoke began to cloud the room. She picked up Paul, grabbed Ivory by the hand and led them out the room though the excessive smoke. They were almost at the door when Ivory pulled away and screamed, "Dolly, sister!

Tanika Lynch

Whore

We gotta get Dolly!"

Kamone's eyes began to water from the smoke as she looked around the room, spotting Ivory's doll lying in front of Cookie's burning body. She put Paul down and sprinted toward the doll. When she bent over to pick it up, Cookie's eyes popped open as she let out the most horrifying squeal and grabbed Kamone's hand, trying to pull her into the burning fire. Kamone screamed in fear as she pulled out her gun and shot Cookie between the eyes. Cookie's screams faded and her body went limp as she took her last and final breath.

Kamone picked Ivory up, put her on one hip, Paul on the other, then ran as fast as she could out the door, down the halls. She was halfway down the staircase when she bumped into Allisa and Honey who were headed up. Kamone stopped in her tracks giving them a stunned look as they did the same. Before they could ask any questions she barged through them and continued running down the stairs.

"What's wrong with that crazy bitch?" Honey laughed, looking over her shoulder curiously.

"Who knows?" Allisa replied, hunching her shoulders as she continued up the stairs, headed to Cookie's place in hopes that she was finished cooking.

"You smell that?" she asked, sniffing the air.

"Smells like somethin' burnin'," Honey replied, now smelling the funny scent in the air as

well.

When they reached the third floor, they were shocked to find fire coming from Cookie's apartment and spreading rapidly down the hall.

"Cookie!" Honey screamed, trying to run toward the fire as Allisa restrained her.

"It's too late!" Allisa cried, choking from the large gray clouds of smoke that filled the air.

"She did it!" Honey yelled frantically as she and Allisa ran down the staircase. "Kamone killed Cookie!"

The two women ran out the apartment screaming about the fire, alerting the other girls that Cookie was trapped inside. Brittany, who had just gotten out of a car with a trick, heard the commotion and came running.

"Cookie dead!" Honey screamed as she saw Brittany making her way through the crowd. "And Kamone killed her! She burnt her up!"

Brittany almost fainted when she heard those words but rage instantly took over.

"Where she at!" Brittany screamed, looking all over the streets. "Where's Kamone at?"

"I seen her and the kids running that way," someone in the crowd answered, pointing down the street.

Brittany put her hands up to her eyes to shield them from the beating sun as she looked for Kamone. From a distance she could see someone running with two small figures on her hips. "There

Tanika Lynch

the bitch go!" Brittany pointed, shouting in a baritone voice. "Get her!"

As Kamone looked over her shoulder, she could see someone running like an African cheetah with a pack of other people behind him. Her heart skipped a beat when she noticed that it was Brittany–she could recognize those long legs anywhere. She knew she had to do something. If Brittany and the others caught up with them they would surely kill Kamone and the kids without a second thought for what she had done to Cookie. She tried running faster but Ivory and Paul weighed her down. Out of fear she ran into traffic and jumped into the back of a car that was driven by an old black man who was just waiting for the light to turn green.

"Help me!" she cried, locking all of the man's car doors. "They're trying to kill us! You gotta help us!"

Before the man could reply, Brittany jumped onto the back end of the car and punched the back window so hard that the entire glass cracked. Before the man knew what happened, a group of women had surrounded his car, screaming obscenities as they kicked, punched and rattled his car, trying to get in.

Ivory and Paul screamed and hid their faces in Kamone's lap as the old man wasted no time pressing the gas pedal to escape the angry mob of hoes.

Kamone held Paul and Ivory tight as she looked

out the back window and saw Brittany still holding on to the trunk. Her long wig blew off as she head-butted the window, still trying to get Kamone. The old man, who saw her as well, made a quick, sharp turn, and continued on as Brittany fell off with a thump, rolling wildly in the middle of the street.

"It's OK now," Kamone said, hugging the kids as they cried uncontrollably. "Nobody's gonna hurt us ever again." She exhaled and sunk down in her seat as she closed her eyes and allowed images of her childhood to flash before her eyes. She saw her father, her mother, Cookie and the hookers she had known all her life, burning within the fires as the old man flew through traffic.

Here she was, homeless, left with two small children. They had little money, no clothes and no family to turn to. Yet, she smiled happily because they were finally free.

Regardless of the negative factor, she knew that life could only get better for them from here. She was a survivor, and she would do whatever had to be done to survive. She looked at the number that was written on the back of her hand, and knew exactly what route she'd take next. She had been used and abused by men all her life. Now, it was her turn.

Tanika Lynch

chapter
twelve

Kamone sat on the edge of the bed counting the money she had taken from Cookie's as Ivory and Paul lay behind her, sleeping like two perfect angels in their hotel bed. Two-thousand and fifty-eight dollars was her total and she knew that would not go far, being that she had to buy them all new clothes, shoes and other necessities they would need.

Plus, they needed food and she had to pay for their room day to day. But on the other hand, she had called Lucci a few seconds ago and told him everything that went down. He was on his way to the hotel and if she had him labeled correctly she knew that all her problems would disappear at his expense. She planned to use him for as long as she could or until she came up with another strategy.

After everything calmed down, Kamone partially explained her situation to the old black man, adding and deleting a few things in order to be seen

as the victim. The man was happy that he had come to the assistance of the young woman and her two small children. He was so taken back by her story that he offered to accompany her to the police station so that he could be her witness to the attempted assault but Kamone declined. Instead, she offered to pay him whatever fee he deemed fit if he would drive them as far away as he could and rent them a hotel room in his name, being that she had apparently lost her ID card in the midst of running from her attackers. The old man was very sympathetic toward her and agreed to help her any why that he could, taking only the money he needed to pay for the room. He even treated the kids to Happy Meals after seeing how excited they became as he passed a McDonald's.

As he drove on, he and Kamone engaged in conversation, or at least he did, as Kamone didn't feel comfortable discussing too much of her business with strangers, after everything she had been though.

He told her his name was Mr. Roberts, and he was the deacon of a church in Detroit's East side area. He was very well known for his prophetic abilities, and he had been on his way to church when she jumped into his car. Being the very deeply religious man that he was, he told her that there was a reason that God had directed her to him out of the many other cars she had the opportunity to jump into.

Tasika Lynch

He talked to her about God and his mercy and grace, but Kamone only pretended to listen. Her mind was too focused on plotting revenge against Brittany and the boys who had raped her. It wasn't until Mr. Roberts began speaking on things that no stranger could possibly know about her that she hung on to every word he said.

As he spoke, she found comfort in his choice of words. No one had ever explained to her in such depth about this man named Jesus. Cookie had read the Bible to her a few times when she was little, but the parts that Cookie read made Kamone fear this unknown being. She steered clear of the bible and anyone who had anything to do with it.

Before they departed, Mr. Roberts invited her to attend his church services and gave her a small pocket bible that he carried in his glove compartment, which contained the name, number and address of the church. He explained to her that the bible was her real weapon in the battles she was both fighting and facing and to fall on her knees and call on the name of Jesus whenever she became discouraged or needed help.

But what almost brought tears to Kamone's eyes was when he looked at her as if in a trance and boldly told her that she was nothing like her mother and the cycle of despair could be broken if she believed and called on Jesus' name. He told her that God was walking her through the valley of death and would bring her out with a better mind

than before. And that her trials and tribulations were not meant to destroy her but to make her stronger. She had to endure such suffering in order to understand the pain in the hearts of the many people God would send to her so that she could save their souls.

Kamone thought about this as she sat slouched over at the foot of the bed. She knew that Mr. Roberts did have some kind of gift. She hadn't told the man a thing about her mother, or any of the other things he spoke on. But she couldn't see herself saving anyone; she was barely saving herself. It all sounded good, but she felt that nothing he said could help change her current situation. Where was God when she was being raped all those times? Where was God when she was hungry? Where was God when Cookie used her love for her siblings against her to make her sell her precious body? But more importantly, where was God now? Her thoughts were interrupted by an impatient knock at the door. She quickly hid her money in the crease of her new bible and placed it into her coat pocket before opening the door.

Lucci rushed in, looking puzzled as he took inventory of the cheap room. "Are you all right, babygirl?" he asked, flicking his cigarette out the door before closing it behind himself.

"Yeah," Kamone replied in a fake faint voice. "We—we all right. Just a little exhausted. That's all." She gave him a slight smile.

Tanika Lynch

Lucci took off his baseball cap and rubbed his hand through his short, naturally curly hair. "Yeah, I bet. It's been a long-ass day for you." Looking down at Paul and Ivory who were still asleep he said, "This must be your brother and sister."

Kamone nodded her head slowly, looking up at him with her puppy dog eyes that made any man melt like butter. "Yeah. Them my babies."

"They didn't see what happened did they?"

Kamone nodded her head in agreement looking away from him as she said, "My baby sister did. Cookie slapped her and busted her lip when she tried to help me. That's why I did what I did."

"Damn, I know they gotta be traumatized," he replied, shaking his head in pity. "Did anybody else see you kill that lady?"

"No. It was just us. I ... I really didn't set the apartment on fire, Lucci. She ... she I ... I mean ..."

"Don't even worry about it," Lucci replied, placing his hand over her lips. "We don't even have to talk about it right now. I just wanted to make sure it wasn't no witnesses out there that could go to the police on you. I feel like it's my fault. I'm the one that gave you that gun. But if I knew you were gonna do all that I woulda' stopped you from even going up in that place."

"It's not your fault. It was bound to happen sooner or later. Somebody had to die. Luckily it wasn't me," Kamone replied, taking a seat back on the edge of the bed.

133

Lucci rubbed his hand over his mouth, tugging at his nicely trimmed goatee as he looked around the room again. "Look," he said, walking over to the bed and picking up Paul. "Grab ya'll stuff and come with me," he ordered, picking up Ivory as well.

"Where we going?" she asked curiously, grabbing Ivory's half-melted doll off the bed. "This room is paid for until tomorrow."

"I can't let ya'll stay up in here." He frowned looking at the dirty comforter on the bed. "The least I can do is give ya'll a decent place to stay. I got a four bedroom house and don't nobody live there but me. I wouldn't feel right leaving ya'll here. Besides, you need some rest. And I'll know you're safe if you're with me."

"Thank you," Kamone said softly, walking over to open up the door for him. "I promise as soon as I get on my feet I'll repay you."

"Don't worry 'bout that," Lucci said, stepping out the door. "Everything in life doesn't cost. Like I said before, there are still good people left in the world. All I ask of you is to be straight up with me at all times. Is that too much to ask?" he asked gazing at her with intense eyes.

"No," Kamone replied, seeing the seriousness of his words in his eyes. "It's not."

"Good," he replied, now walking toward his maroon-colored Benz. "We'll get along just fine then."

Tanika Lynch

Whore

There is a God, she thought to herself, smelling the wonderful scent of expensive leather as she opened his car door. She closed her eyes and sank down into the butter-soft leather seats, thanking whoever it was up there above those big blue clouds that allowed her to meet this man. Her plan was going better than expected. She just hoped she could play on his sympathy long enough for her to come up with a plan B.

Tanika Lynch

Triple Crown Publications presents . . .

Tanika Lynch

chapter
thirteen

"Ivory, I want you to be on your best behavior for Yolanda," Kamone ordered, pulling Ivory's long locks back into a ponytail as they sat on the living room couch. "When we come pick ya'll up I better not hear about you sneakin' snacks in the middle of the night again or no more dolls for you," she threatened.

"I'll be good this time, sister," Ivory replied, kissing each one of her new Barbie dolls as she placed them into her overnight bag. "But what if Yolanda's ugly daughter hits me again?" she asked, frowning as she turned to face Kamone.

"Every time we go over there, Ne-Ne and Ramel always tryin' to take me and Paul's toys."

"Ne-Ne and Ramel is ya'll friends and friends share," Kamone explained. "And if they do something you don't like, tell their mama. No fighting."

"Sister, did you know Ne-Ne jealous of me cuz I gotta long ponytail and hers little?" Ivory said, bat-

ting her long lashes as she shook her ponytail.

"And you jealous of her because her stomach little and yours ain't," Kamone joked, poking Ivory in the belly. "That goes for you, too, Paul," Kamone turned her attention to Paul who lay in the middle of the floor crashing his toy cars together. "You ain't innocent like you pretend to be. No fighting. You hear me?"

Paul nodded his head in agreement, not bothering to look up as he continued to make pretend engine noises.

"Come on ya'll." Kamone jumped to her feet and grabbed their bags when she heard Yolanda's horn beeping. "Yolanda's here."

Paul jumped up, carrying his cars under his arm as he struggled to put on his jacket while Ivory pouted, dragging her feet across the floor.

"Sister, I don't wanna go," she whined. "Why can't I go to the party? I love Lucci, too."

"Only grown people can go," Kamone explained, helping Paul to put on his jacket.

"You not a grown up. Why you can go then?" Ivory asked, rolling her neck in a sassy manner.

"Cuz I'm growner than you. That's why I can go then," Kamone laughed, imitating Ivory's neck roll as she gave the two a kiss on the cheek.

"I wove you," Paul said, softly kissing Kamone back before running out the door behind Ivory.

"I love you, too, baby." Kamone smiled, following them out the door and standing on the porch to

Tanika Lynch

wave at Yolanda.

"What's up, boo?" Yolanda yelled as she opened the door to her newest Land Rover truck and allowed the kids in. "Tell my cousin I said happy birthday."

"All right girl." Kamone smiled. "When the baby due?"

"Thirty-eight days and counting," Yolanda answered, rubbing her protruding stomach. "As soon as I drop it, we hittin' the club so I can show off my new truck," she said, doing a little dance in her seat before closing the door.

Kamone giggled and waved goodbye as Yolanda drove off, shaking her head as she noticed Ne-Ne and Ivory already going at it in the backseat.

Yolanda, who was Lucci's favorite girl cousin, was the only person Kamone trusted to baby-sit Paul and Ivory. Yolanda had two children around the same ages with another on the way. She and Kamone had become close, and Yolanda treated them just like family.

Kamone had been living with Lucci for close to two months now, and he had her feeling back on top of the world. The day after they moved in with him, he took down all their sizes, and returned hours later with more clothes and footwear than all three of them had ever owned put together. And none of the stuff he bought was cheap.

His four bedroom home looked like something out of a magazine to Kamone. It was decked out

with only the finest things from the attic to the basement. There was a patio and a built in pool in his huge backyard, and he owned more cars than he could park in his three car garage.

Paul and Ivory bonded instantly with Lucci, and he spoiled the two rotten. Every morning, he would allow Kamone to rest while he got up early to feed and dress the kids. Everywhere he went, unless he was taking care of his business, he took them, allowing Kamone the time he thought she needed to herself. Lucci was very fond of the kids, and never corrected strangers who complimented him on fathering the fine looking pair. Paul did some-what resemble him, and Ivory was the kind of little girl that would make any man proud to call his own.

As for Kamone, he treated her like a queen. She didn't have to do anything but study two hours out the day with the tutors he had hired to catch Kamone, Ivory and even Paul up on their education. Lucci had his own personal house keeper, who came in each morning and did everything from the dishes to the grocery shopping.

Lucci often took them to amusement parks, out to eat and other places they had never been. And when he left the house alone, he never returned without some kind of gift for them. He surely had a heart of gold, and was a man of remarkable character.

Lucci was a well-established man on the streets

Tanika Lynch

known for having the purest blow and cocaine around. He also ran a few pill and weed houses on the East, West and Southwest sides of Detroit. None of his dope spots or connections ever got busted, thanks to his brother and several other dirty Detroit cops that he paid off swell. And if he or any of his partners ever ran into any trouble, his big-shot attorney father was so good in law that he could get off a man who committed a triple homicide in front of the police. The big shots called him Mr. Big and he was just as dirty as his sons.

* * *

As time went by, Kamone developed a physical attraction for Lucci and she knew the feeling had to be mutual although they had never even kissed and slept in separate rooms. They did everything a couple did, yet other than an occasional hug, no physical contact was involved.

Kamone tried coming on to him once thinking that she had to give him sex in order for him to continue providing for herself and the kids. But Lucci turned her down, telling her that she was too young for him and he wasn't helping her in hopes of sex, but because he had more than enough to share and she deserved to see the brighter side of life that he knew she never had. He explained to her that she no longer had to use her body in order to survive and that she should wait to have sex

with someone she truly loved.

Kamone was both grateful and offended at the same time. She was happy to know that Lucci was not like other men she had met and did the things he did from the kindness of his heart. Yet no man had ever turned her away and her feelings got caught up in what started out as a game to her. She had deep feelings for Lucci. He was everything any girl could want. Tall, dark, handsome, intelligent, kind, ghetto rich and didn't mind spending. Even though no women called the house and he never spoke of any women in his life, she knew that as gorgeous as he was, he probably had women all over. But being the man that he was he not only respected his home but the feelings that he knew Kamone had for him.

Kamone tried her best to show Lucci that she was mature beyond her years, in hopes that it would change his mind, but she had a hunch that her past history had something to do with why he wouldn't touch her. He knew all about her using drugs and hooking but all that was behind her now.

Kamone took an occasional drink with Lucci, and, other than the bad habit of smoking Newport '00s that she picked up from him, she was as clean as a whistle. Her main goal had become making Lucci her man. She knew that if she didn't hook him it was always the possibility that another woman could steal him away, taking all her good fortune with him. And she wasn't about to let that

Tanika Lynch

happen. She wanted to give herself to him in a bad way, but he just wouldn't take the bait. Kamone often wondered if he was either seriously involved with someone or possibly even gay and just didn't have the heart to tell her. But whatever he was she was determined to make him hers, by hook or crook, more sooner than later.

When Lucci arrived home from running errands, he and Kamone began preparing for his and David's big birthday bash that was being thrown at a nightclub called The Platinum.

Lucci stepped out in style, wearing his cream tailored Armani suit. It was topped off with a sharp-collared, sapphire, pure silk Armani shirt with the matching sapphire hanky, neatly folded in his suit coat pocket and matching sapphire-colored big block gators on his feet. The sapphire-tinted Cartier glasses he wore brought attention to his well-groomed face and hair. He set it all off with a diamond-filled platinum chain draped around his neck, a diamond-filled platinum Rolex watch and two diamond pinky rings that were big enough to blind a room full of people alone. Lucci was GQ material and he knew it.

His eyes sparkled like stars when Kamone came out her room wearing her elegant, silk, sapphire-colored backless Roberto Cavalli dress which wrapped around her neck with a V slant in the front that stopped right before her belly button. The bottom part flowed into a downward slant and the dress hugged her body like wet plastic showing all curves. Her sapphire-colored Manolo Blahnik jeweled stilettos showed off her beautifully manicured toes and brought definition to her flawless legs. She wore her hair silky straight, to the back, allowing everyone to see her naturally beautiful face and heart-shaped diamond studded earrings that Lucci had recently given her.

She was taken aback when Lucci walked up behind her and slipped a platinum, diamond and sapphire crushed necklace with a heart-shaped diamond pendent onto her neck, along with a matching tennis bracelet. She had never imagined having such beautiful things, but it was something that she could get used to.

When they pulled into the parking lot of the club, which they had rented out for the night, it was already jam-packed and more cars were arriving. She knew that all of Lucci's big ballin' friends were expected to be here, and some of his family as well. This would be her first time meeting them all, and she wanted everyone to like her.

Even though Lucci had her looking like a million bucks, in reality, she was still just a young chick from the slums with a real bad reputation. She walked in holding Lucci's arm tight, too ashamed to tell him about her insecurities. As soon as they entered, people began chanting his name as women swarmed him and pulled him in different directions, leaving Kamone standing alone to min-

Tanika Lynch

gle by herself.

She took a seat at the bar, ordering drink after drink, as she jealously watched Lucci being sandwiched on the dance floor by beautiful older women. But it was his night, he was the man of the hour, and who was she to spoil it?

She was sitting there, playing with the straw in her glass of tequila when Lucci grabbed her hand and danced his way back to the dance floor with her.

"You thought I forgot about you?" He smiled, pulling her close and grinding his body into hers. "How could I when you're the prettiest girl here?"

Kamone giggled softly, feeling much better knowing that she was on his mind.

"For a minute I thought you forgot," she replied, feeling a sprint of confidence as all the women watched them jealously, probably wondering who she was.

They were on their third song when David, who had just arrived, spotted Lucci and ran over to him, playfully punching him in the side.

"Happy birthday, nigga!" David laughed, dressed just as sharp as Lucci with a bottle of imported Cristal champagne in his hand.

"Happy birthday to you, too, old man," Lucci joked, giving him a hand pound before they embraced. "I thought you wasn't gonna make it. They said you have to do some overtime on the job."

"What?" David laughed. "Fuck that job and fuck the police. Nigga ain't nothin' mo' important than our birthday." David turned up his bottle as he glanced over at Kamone, doing a double-take with a peculiar look on his face.

"Damn," he said, looking her up and down, removing his Burberry frames. "We met before, Ma?"

"Oh," Lucci said as he placed his arm around Kamone. "This is a very good friend of mine. Her name is Kamone. Kamone, this is evidently my twin brother."

"Kamone," he repeated, trying to remember how he knew her.

"Hey," Lucci interrupted, sensing her discomfort. "That lil' Asian chick Tekey been askin' about you all night, dog. I think she gotta gift for you."

"Freaky Tekey?" David questioned, showing interest. "I bet that bitch do got a gift for me after I didn't arrest her when I caught her with all that stolen merchandise. Boooy, I swear Tekey give the best head," he laughed, cupping his penis. "Where she at?"

"I just seen her sittin' at the bar with Nikki."

"Nasty Nikki?" David replied, rolling his eyes into the back of his head as if remembering the pleasure. "Let me go see what I can get in to. You comin'?"

"Naw, man. Go on and handle yo' business. I'll be right here," Lucci replied, encouraging him to

Tanika Lynch

leave.

David took another good look at Kamone as he walked off, knowing for sure that he had seen that pretty face somewhere before.

Kamone stood with her arms folded and her head hung low feeling defeated. She knew that she had been just seconds away from being discovered and having her filthy past thrown in her face had Lucci not distracted David's train of thought.

Lucci stood over Kamone, placing his finger under her chin and lifting her head to make her look him in the eyes. "I know you not gonna allow one ignorant fool tear you down like this. You've come too far. Hold yo' head up and be proud of who you are now. Not who you used to be. I know I'm proud of you," he added with a sexy smile. "I know everything I need to know about you. Can't nobody tell me shit."

Kamone stared at Lucci for a moment, taking in his words before giving him a sideways smile and wrapping her arms around his neck. "Don't leave me," she whispered, squeezing him tight.

"I won't," he replied, hugging her back. From that point on, Lucci kept Kamone glued to his side. He knew that he was her protector and he didn't mind having the title of her super hero nor did he care who had something to say about it. He enjoyed being in her company and she caught every eye in the club.

After what turned out to be a wonderful night,

Lucci and Kamone said their goodbyes to everyone, leaving earlier than to be expected. They were laughing and joking with each other as they headed through the parking lot to Lucci's white Viper GTS when David, who was standing in the lot talking with several women, spotted them.

"Hey, Lucci!" he yelled, putting the women on hold and running over to his brother. "Where you going?" he asked, snatching Lucci's cigarette from his lips and taking a drag.

"I'm out, dog. It's been beautiful but I got thangs to do in the morning," he explained as he pushed his alarm button.

"Nigga, you startin' to act yo' age," David laughed, throwing the cigarette to the ground and lighting the blunt he had placed behind his ear. "I had plans for us, son." He held a mouth full of smoke as he pointed back at the group of sexy women. "I thought we'd party like we used to. Take our birthday out with a bang, for old times' sake." He grinned, nudging Lucci's side.

"I'm tight on that," Lucci sailed. "Gone and knock it out for us both, playboy. Call me in the morning. Maybe we can hook up and exchange gifts or somethin'."

David turned his lips downward, nodding his head up and down as he looked back and forth at Kamone and Lucci. "I'll do that," he replied, taking another puff.

"But, um, before you roll out, let me holla at

Tanika Lynch

you, hermano to hermano."

Kamone picked up on the hint, and walked on to get into the car. She sat there, watching out the rearview mirror as the two talked behind the car. When she noticed that David's body language had become aggressive, and heard Lucci raising his voice a notch, she quietly rolled down the window to be nosey, wondering what the two could be arguing about on their birthday.

"Lucci, listen to me, dog, that girl's bad news. I know all about that bitch. She's a junkie, and an indigent booty-sellin' bitch! You don't know what you gettin' into fuckin' wit' a bitch like that. And ain't no brotha' of mine gone be sportin' no scanty bitch like that. And you got her livin' wit' you too, man? Please don't tell me you done told that bitch none of our business."

"Chill, man," Lucci said softly, putting his hand on his brother's shoulder. "It's not even like that, OK? She's not my woman, first of all. She's had a hard time in life, and I'm just lookin' out for her and her kid brother and sister."

"Get rid of that penny-pinchin' bitch, dog. Let another nigga feel sorry for her. I heard she's dangerous, and a snake. You can't trust a low-lifed bitch like her. You'll fuck around and wake up to a empty house, and the FBI bustin' through the door."

"David," Lucci chuckled, "I got this. Don't worry about me, baby bubba. Ole girl is harmless.

149

She's really a sweet kid."

Kamone held back her tears as she rolled up the window. She had heard enough. She knew this was all too good to be true. How dare she believe for one moment that a man like Lucci could ever want a dusty, poor bitch like herself. She quickly wiped away a fallen tear as David and Lucci embraced once more before departing.

Lucci hopped in, lighting himself a cigarette before starting up his engine. He looked over at Kamone, blowing smoke out his nose, as he said, "My brother's really comical, huh?"

"Yeah, a real fuckin' knee-slapper," she growled.

"What's wrong with you?" Lucci asked, unaware that she overheard their conversation. Kamone twisted her lips and rolled her eyes as she flipped him off. Lucci chuckled, hunching his shoulders as he turned on the radio. He figured she was mad that David invited him to a night of sex with all those women.

It wasn't until he pulled up into the garage of his home and turned to make a joke with Kamone that he noticed her face was all wet from the silent tears she had shed the entire way home.

"What's wrong, babygirl?" he asked, wrinkles creasing his forehead as he reached out and touched her face.

Kamone jerked away, wheezing heavily as she frowned at him though mascara-smudged eyes.

Tanika Lynch

"Don't touch me!" she declared. "I wouldn't want your royal hands to get dusty," she commented sarcastically before jumping out the car and running into the house through the side door.

"What'd I do?" he asked, completely dumbfounded as he jumped out the car, running after her. "Kamone!" he yelled in a thunderous tone, grabbing her by the arm as she entered the living room. "What's the deal, girl? Why you trippin'?"

"You tell me what the deal is!" she wailed, snatching her arm away. "Oh, I know. You're to good to fuck with a ugly, uninformed, shabby bitch like me!"

"What? Where did that come from? I've never insulted you."

"Letting your arrogant-ass brother talk about me was insulting enough!" she shouted. "I heard everything. David made me feel like shit, and you just stood there talkin' like I was a charity case. David was just saying what you think. That's why you won't touch me. You think I'm a disgusting junkie whore, don't you?"

"No!" he shouted back. "I ... I don't hold your past against you, Kamone. Fuck David and what he thinks. If it wasn't for my business in the streets, I wouldn't have shit to do with him. You don't really know how I feel about him. And I surely don't value shit he has to say!"

"You won't even confess your feelings for me. You made sure he knew I wasn't your woman.

151

Explaining to him how I had a hard life. Why didn't you just tell him everything? Tell him how my incestuous father was my HIV infected mother's pimp. Why didn't you tell him how you found me in the trash, all doped up, beat up and raped? Or how I came to live with you after killing the bitch that..."

Before Kamone could finish, Lucci grabbed her and hugged her tight, burying her head in his chest. She became weak at the knees as she broke down into deep sobs letting it all out.

"I'm so sorry," he whispered as tears ran rapidly down his face down into her hair. "I never meant to hurt you. All I ever wanted to do was make you happy."

"Do you even love me?" she asked, tilting her head sideways on his chest.

"If I didn't you wouldn't be here."

"It's either yes or no," she replied, pushing away from him and backing up toward the couch. "I need to know. I need to hear you say it."

Lucci took a long breath, looking at Kamone as she awaited his answer. "Yeah I love you, Kamone. I've loved you from the day I laid eyes on you."

"Why won't you claim me then?" she asked, looking like a baby in the face.

"Because you're young and I don't want to abuse you like other men in your life. Love isn't sex. Fuckin' isn't love. You make love when you're in love and I don't wanna fuck you."

Tanika Lynch

Whore

"Well," she began, unsnapping the back of her dress and letting it fall to the floor, "make love to me then. That is, if you feel the same."

Lucci stood there slowly shaking his head, inspecting Kamone's voluptuous body. Her skin looked softer than the silk dress she stepped out of and her nipples stood to attention like soldiers on her perky breasts. Her stomach lay flat and smooth and her fat vagina bared only a thin strip of hair down the center.

His mind was telling him, *No, she is still merely a child,* but his body spoke for itself as his manhood began to rise within his silk cream boxers.

"Make me feel beautiful," she begged, shaking her hair out before falling to the floor and crawling over to him like a heated leopard. "Make me a woman," she whispered, slowly rubbing up the sides of his legs as she teased his stiff penis with her lips and tongue as it grew to its capacity down the leg of his pants.

Lucci was stuck, trying so hard to fight the feeling, but his penis throbbed like a beating heart as her wet tongue soiled the crotch of his pants. She gave him no choice but to crave her. He had to satisfy his appetite.

"I'm not a child," she said softly, unzipping his pants with her teeth and helping them to slide down his muscular legs onto his ankles. "I can make you feel better than any woman you've ever been with," she proclaimed, flickering her tongue

along the print of his penis.

Lucci developed a lump in his throat, swallowing hard, becoming mesmerized by her passion-filled eyes and feeling hypnotized by her delicate touch.

Kamone slowly unbuttoned his jacket, threw it to the floor and tore off his shirt, revealing his glistening buffed chest and six-packed stomach. Kamone pulled down his boxers, constantly looking into his eyes as she deep throated his long, thick, juicy penis.

Lucci quickly peeled off his shoes and stepped out of his clothes as he rocked back and forth in her mouth. He grabbed the back of her head and slow grinded all the way down her throat. His eyes rolled into the back of his head and he let out a loud grunt as a sensual feeling surged throughout his entire body. He couldn't take it any more. He had to have her!

He pulled her head back, stood her up by her arms and began outlining her lips with the tip of his soft tongue. His hands massaged her breasts, allowing her nipples to rest in the creases of his fingers, caressing them lustfully. He picked her up and made her wrap her legs around his neck as he licked her female juices, darting his tongue in and out of her hole. He grabbed a hold of her clitoris with his lips, and sucked it as he would the juices from a peach. Kamone whimpered in pleasure from this feeling she had never felt before, and within

Tanika Lynch

seconds, she shook and cried out in orgasm.

Lucci quickly lowered her down to his hips, and wasted no time boldly slamming his 11 inches inside of her. Her vagina gripped his penis like a magnet, as if suction cups had been placed on the sides and base of her vagina. His loud moaning overtook hers as he bounced her up and down, walking toward the couch. He sat down and allowed her to ride him like a stallion as he gripped her butt cheeks and spread them apart to get more of himself inside of her.

All the while, David, who had followed them home without their knowledge, stood outside on the porch, watched them through the open blinds and masturbated to the live freak show.

He had planned on acting like he had dropped by to have a few drinks alone with Lucci, to finish off their birthday. But in actuality, he had really come by with intentions of getting a better look at Kamone, since Lucci put it out there that she wasn't his woman. To his unexpected delight, he got the view of his life!

He had been standing there from the moment the arguing began; he had heard everything that was said and he was hot under the collar by Lucci's comments but it was all good.

As he stroked himself, he jealously imagined himself inside of Kamone's hot nest instead of Lucci. He had wanted a piece of Kamone ever since their first encounter and watching the way she

rolled her hips on his brother's dick like that made him want her even more. He could feel her wetness, taste her skin and smell her scent as he whacked away like there was no tomorrow. When Lucci growled out in orgasm, so did he, allowing his seeds to splatter all across the window and the cement porch.

His imagination still ran wild even after busting a healthy nut, and the only way that it could be satisfied was if he had her himself. Now that he had a little unknown dirt on her and he had heard for himself how his beloved brother really felt about him, all was fair in love and war!

David had every intention on going after what was rightfully his at all costs. He wanted Kamone for himself and just the thought of Lucci tearing his pussy up the way he had tonight made his black heart tick a little bit faster!

Tanika Lynch

chapter
fourteen

"Brother," Ivory called out to Lucci from the backseat. "Is cheesecake gonna be at the place you takin' us to? I love me some cheesecake."

"I don't remember," Lucci laughed, keeping his eyes on the road. "I think they might serve it. But if they don't, we'll stop at the store on the way home and get you one all to yourself," he promised. "You want one too, pimp daddy?" he asked, looking through his rearview mirror at Paul, who sat quietly playing with the rim of his baseball cap.

"Paul don't like cheesecake," Ivory answered. "I'll just eat his for him."

"Ivory what I tell you 'bout being so greedy?" Kamone interrupted, looking back at her sister. "You goin' on eight years old and you already weigh more than me. And stop answering for Paul. He can speak for his self."

"Awww," Lucci smiled, looking back at Ivory

as she pouted. "Stop talkin' like that to my piggy baby, you big meanie!" he joked with Kamone.

"Yeah, you big meanie," Ivory repeated, hitting the back of Kamone's seat.

"Pimp daddy is a real pimp. He don't like talkin', so Ivory do it for him."

"I want pickles," Paul shouted out, making everyone burst into laughter.

"That's what I like about you, pimp daddy. You a simple man," Lucci chuckled.

"What's that smell?" Kamone frowned, sniffing in what smelled like rotten eggs.

"Ivory!" Paul yelled, pointing at his sister. "Her farted," he said in a cute baby voice.

"You did!" Ivory shouted back, pointing the finger at Paul.

"And see he ain't stupid," Lucci laughed. "He know how to throw the weight off on other people."

"Ya'll so nasty," Kamone laughed, turning off the air conditioner and rolling down the windows. "Whoever it was, you smell like a dirty old pig."

"Piggy baby," Paul giggled, pointing at Ivory again.

"Speaking of gas," Lucci said, changing lanes. "I need to stop and fill up the tank."

Lucci pulled into a local gas station in the Eight Mile area before heading to the Rooster Tail, where the four planned to have lunch before

Tanika Lynch

they headed to Six Flags and then to the Fox Theater where they were going to see Cinderella live.

Lucci was flying out to California the next morning with a few of his partners to seal a deal on another connection, and since he planned on being gone for a whole week, he wanted to make his last day with them special.

Kamone sat in the car, playing with the radio when a homely-looking couple ran up to Lucci's Benz. "Can me and my old lady clean yo' widows real good foe a lil' bit of spare change?" the shabby-looking, hot-breathed black man asked, sticking his ugly sunken face into Kamone's window and giving her a toothless smile as he held a blue spray bottle and squeegee in his shaky, puffy, abscess-infected hands.

Kamone, who had been startled by the pair, clenched her chest, leaned over toward the driver's seat, and frowned as she looked into his deformed face.

"Yea ... yeah," she answered, looking back to see that the woman already began to wipe the back window. "Go ahead."

"Good lookin'." He smiled, starting on the front window shield. "This sho' nuff a nice ride." He stuck his face against the window as he cleaned it to get a better look inside.

Kamone took a breath of relief when she saw Lucci walking out the station with two packs of

bubble gum.

"This here you?" the man asked Lucci as he approached.

"Yeah," Lucci replied, looking the man over as he leaned into the window handing Ivory and Paul the gum. "What's this?" he asked, smirking at Kamone before glancing at the man then back at the woman who took her sweet time cleaning the back window.

"They ran up on the car and asked if they could do our windows for a few dollars." Kamone laughed.

"Can I pump that gas for a little extra?" the woman asked, scratching her skinny arms and looking pitifully at Lucci.

"Go right ahead," Lucci replied, trying to hold back his laughter, checking out her outfit as he got into the car.

"All done." The man smacked Lucci's hood as he checked out his work.

"You hooked it up, my man," Lucci remarked, going into his pocket and handing a 20-dollar bill out to the man.

"Oh, hell naw!" the homely-looking white woman yelled, running and snatching the money up. "I'm holding it this time, nigga," she declared, stuffing the money into her dingy yellow sock.

As the woman spoke, Kamone paid her closer attention, realizing that her voice sounded famil-

Tanika Lynch

iar. She observed the woman as she stood by the driver's side arguing over the money. Even though she was probably in her early 30s, she looked much, much older. She had red blotches and old scars covering her acne-filled, malnourished face. Huge bags hung under her dull green eyes and every last tooth in her mouth was gone, making her slur every word. Her greasy thinning blond hair was held back in a stringy ponytail by a dirty pink ribbon and even though she probably weighed less than 80 pounds, she had the nerves to be wearing a skimpy, holey green tank top and cut off blue jean booty shorts. She looked terrible, but there was no doubt about it to Kamone. The woman was her mother.

"Suga," Kamone called out softly, praying to God that she didn't answer back.

The woman whipped her head toward the car, squinting as she looked inside, wondering who in the world could know her driving around in such a fancy vehicle.

Suga's mouth dropped open as her bad vision focused in on Kamone. "Ladybug?" she gasped, calling her by the nickname she had given her. "Ladybug, that's you?" she squealed, running around to Kamone's side. "Oh my Jesus!" she said joyously, throwing her hands up to her mouth as she looked in the back seat at Paul and Ivory. "I can't believe it!" she shouted, snatching the back door open and jumping in to hug the

kids. "Peanut!" she called out to her man. "These here all my kids! These my babies!"

"Go'n on, you crazy bitch," Peanut replied, flapping his hand at her. "Ain't no way in hell a broke junkie bitch like you know these rich folk. And they certainly ain't yo' kin."

Lucci looked at Kamone in utter shock as she looked back at him in shame, disgust and humiliation.

Paul and Ivory squirmed in their seats, smelling their mother's horrible body odor as she hugged and kissed them all over their faces. "Ya'll remember me? Ya'll remember mama?" she asked excitedly. "Ya'll done got just as big."

"Mama," Kamone called out, jumping out the car to get Suga's attention, so that her dirty, infected ass could stop kissing and touching the kids. "Mama, where you been?"

Suga jumped out, grabbed Kamone's hands and gripped them tight as she took a good look at her. "Ladybug, you done got to be so beautiful. You always was though," she said as she bent over to peek inside the car, waving excitedly at Lucci. "That there yo' pimp, ladybug?" she whispered, shooting Lucci a flirtatious wink, as her thin, bumpy lips blew him a kiss.

"No, mama. He's my boyfriend," Kamone answered, shaking her head as she looked at the disgusting open sores on Suga's legs.

"I heard all 'bout you, babygirl. Um huh. They

Tanika Lynch

say you was makin' a killin' on the streets. I say to myself, my baby just like her mama. I knew you'd make it big one day wit' that pretty face. But I'll have you know, you got that good pussy from me." She laughed.

"Mama, where you been?" Kamone repeated, more out of curiosity than concern.

"Well," Suga began, scratching her leg with her foot, like a stray dog. "After I left I bumped into a girl from my hometown. She told me my pa wasn't dead. She say a neighbor boy of ours seen me and Spice runnin' from that burnin' house and he went and saved pa." Suga stood bouncing from leg to leg. She seemed jittery, as if she needed a fix. She scratched herself all over and picked at her open sores as she spoke. "So you know I was still mad wit' him for what he did to me and Spice as kids–ya know? It was cuz of him our lives were all fucked up. So I seen it fit to head back on down there and get him good this time for what he done to us. I hitchhiked my way back home to Alabama, headed to pa's trailer and 'tended like I wasn't mad with him and it was Spice's idea to burn up the house. And you know what, ladybug? Pa hadn't changed a bit. He was still a racist drunk old rednecked pervert. I gave that bastard the fuckin' of his life. That way I knew this time he'd die. I fucked his old ass every day and it didn't take long for the old bastard to die, being he was already sick with cancer

and all that. I gave him AIDS for Spice and my colored children I knew he'd hated had I brought ya'll with me.

"You know I hate men, ladybug. And I didn't feel the least bit guilty for fuckin' the whole community down there." Suga laughed to herself in thought as she wiped the snot that dripped from her nose and wiped it on her shorts. "After that, I headed on back down here with a pocket full of money and that's when I met Peanut." She smiled looking over at the man as he stood scratching like he had fleas.

"That so good to me, ladybug. We stay with his grandma in her basement. She remind me a bit of that bitch, Cookie. She don't see me fit for her Peanut. But Peanut loves me and don't care what I got." She smiled. "I've changed so much, ladybug. I see life differently now thanks to Peanut. I thought about coming back to get ya'll but Peanut thought it would be best if we waited 'til his grandmammie died. Hell, she got one foot in the grave already." She laughed. "And soon, we'll have the house all to ourselves. That way we can live like a real family 'pose to."

"Stop all that jaw jackin', bitch!" Peanut yelled, scratching out of control. "See if you can get some more money from the broad, being she yo' daughter and all. I ain't had a fix all morning, and my stomach bubblin'," he said, frowning down his crusty lips and letting out a loud fart as

Tanika Lynch

he scratched the hair bumps in his nappy beard.

"You show some respect for my kids, ya hear?" Suga yelled back, ice grilling the man.

Kamone looked back and forth at the two as if she were having a nightmare. She couldn't believe this was happening.

"Well, mama," she said, slowly backing away, "we gotta go now. I'm glad to hear you doing so good."

"Wait a minute, ladybug," Suga smiled, reaching out to hug Kamone with bits of blood and pus under her long, yellow nails from picking at her sores.

"Give yo' mama some suga," she requested, puckering up her nasty-looking lips.

A look of horror crossed Kamone's face as she quickly backed away and jumped into the car. "I … I'm sorry, ma, but we running late," she lied.

Suga's whole attitude changed within the blink of an eye as she leaned down onto the window, looking at Kamone as if she were the devil himself. "You ain't changed a bit eitha', you selfish lil' bitch!" she snarled through clenched teeth.

"You still think you betta' than me, huh? Like yo' shit don't stank. Look at you in yo' fancy clothes riding around in yo' fancy car, wit' yo' fancy older man, and draggin' my babies around like they yourin'! This was suppose to be me!" she shouted, slamming her fist down. "This 'pose

165

to be my life!"

"Ma ... mama, here," Kamone whined, feeling like the helpless little girl she once was as she rambled through her purse. "Take it," she said, handing her a fist full of bills. "It's all I can do for ..."

"You think you can buy me!" Suga yelled, snatching the money with speed. "You think this is enough to buy my life? My kids? You always wanted to be me, ya dumb bitch!"

"I've heard enough of this bullshit!" Lucci barked, frowning hard as he started up his car. "Take the money, bitch, and scram! They don't need yo' worthless ass for a muthafuckin' thang! These are our kids now, and Kamone don't wanna be like you, bitch! You ain't no role model. What the fuck you got she wants?"

"Nigga, you stay outta this foe I do to yo' black ass what I did to my pa!" Suga shouted, working up her dry mouth to spit.

Lucci saw it coming, and quickly threw his car into drive. He sped off, running over Suga's feet with his back tires. "Crazy bitch!" he yelled, looking back to see Peanut snatching the money out of Suga's hands as she lay on the ground, holding her feet.

Kamone's head was spinning as she sat in a daze, not hearing anything before she broke down crying. Ivory and Paul, who had been quiet throughout the whole ordeal, began crying as

Tanika Lynch

well, watching their sister cry.

"Aww, man," Lucci said, softly placing his arm around Kamone and looking back at the kids as he continued to drive. "Don't cry ya'll," he said, looking back and forth between them and the road. "Everything's OK now. She never gonna hurt ya'll again."

"I don't want that mama no more," Ivory screamed through her sobs.

"Me either," Paul whined, drooling at the mouth. "Her bad!"

"Ya'll don't have that mama no more," Lucci said softly. "Ya'll got me and your sister. We love ya'll more than anything."

"Can you and sister be our new mama and daddy?" Ivory whimpered, wiping her tears and Paul's tears at the same time.

Ivory's words hit Lucci like an arrow in the heart, making his eyes all watery and red. But he held it in, knowing he had to be strong for them in their time of need.

"We are ya'll mama and daddy," he answered in a crackling voice holding Kamone tighter as she lay against his side, staring blankly with silent tears rolling along her blush red cheeks.

"Thank you, new daddy," Ivory sniffled, standing up in the backseat to grab Lucci's head and kiss his cheek, doing the same to Kamone, as Paul followed behind.

Kamone exhaled, coming out of the state she

was in when she felt the warm loving kisses they gave to her. She wiped her face and grabbed them both, pulling them into her lap and hugging them tightly to her chest. She looked at Lucci with the saddest eyes, still at a loss for words.

"Don't look back, babygirl," he said, caressing her face with the back of his hand. "Don't let the past break you down. It's behind you and gonna stay behind you. You've come to far to fall off now," he said. "Fuck all that shit! We not gonna allow nobody to ruin our day. We still gonna have fun, right?" he yelled, grinning from ear to ear.

"Yeeeah!" Ivory and Paul screamed together, smiling as if nothing had ever happened as they smacked on their watermelon bubble gum.

"Right?" he smiled, touching Kamone's hair as he looked into her eyes.

Kamone bit her bottom lip, giving him a vulnerable smile as she nodded in agreement.

"That's what I'm talkin' about." He grinned, seeing a little life sparking back into her eyes.

The four carried on with their plans as scheduled but Kamone was unusually quiet and very withdrawn all day long. Lucci tried everything possible to cheer her up but nothing seemed to work.

He knew she had to be feeling a wave of emotions, especially anger. Seeing her mother all messed up like that had to have brought back some terrible memories.

Tanika Lynch

Whore

The trip he had planned for the next day was very important to him but he didn't want to leave her alone feeling the way she did. He was afraid she might relapse or even worse, hurt herself.

In an instant, Lucci came up with an idea that would possibly change all of their lives.

Triple Crown Publications presents . . .

Tanika Lynch

chapter
fifteen

"Here," Lucci said, handing Kamone the crystal goose-necked wine glass as she sat in the bubbling Jacuzzi tub. "You need this."

"Thank you," she replied, softly butting her cigarette in the ash tray that sat on the tub's side.

"The kids are stretched out like Jesus on the cross," Lucci chuckled, stepping into the water. "They had a lot of fun today, especially at Six Flags."

"At least somebody did," she said as she cuddled up next to Lucci and closed her eyes.

"Baby," he began, taking a sip from his glass, "I felt your pain today when all that shit went down. It's like our heart became one and when you cried so did I. I've never seen you so hurt and I never want to see it again."

"And ..."

"Wait," he interrupted, putting up his hand. "Let me finish. I was doing some heavy thinking all

day after that and I decided it would be best if we all left Detroit. We both have experienced a lot of messed up shit here. And it's time to leave all this shit behind and make a fresh start."

"But what about all your business?" Kamone asked, looking at him in astonishment. "And what about your family and all your friends?"

"I'm tired of the game," he replied, taking another drink. "I mean it's been good to me, and brought me big bucks. But along with those big bucks came drama and confusion. I'm tired of drama and confusion, and it wouldn't hurt me in the least to step out the game. Flat out, game ova'. I'm sittin' on tons of illegal money. and I think it would be wise of me to invest in some legit business. I mean, I'm only protected by the state boys, not the federal government. At any time, I could get busted. They could take everything. And my life with you and the kids means more to me than slangin' kilos. We can still live phat legally. And as far as friends and family goes, you, Ivory and Paul are the only friends and family I need. If I went for broke right now, ya'll the only ones that would stick by me. My so-called partners and family wouldn't want shit to do wit' me, other than my pops. I ain't no fool. I know how shit goes."

"Where do you want to go?" Kamone asked, playing with the lavender-smelling bathwater.

"I was thinking maybe we could move to Georgia, and do some slow livin' in the South. It

Tanika Lynch

would be a change from the big city. Or, I was thinkin' about checkin' out California while I'm down there, to see what they livin' like. We could get a house built from the ground up by the water somewhere."

"Lucci," Kamone began, looking up at him as she rubbed his smooth chest. "Why do you love me so much?"

Lucci looked at Kamone, shaking his head slowly before throwing back the rest of his drink. "You remind me a lot of my mama," he answered, sitting his glass down. "Strong, outgoing, beautiful and she would give her life for her kids. I was a mama's boy."

"Why haven't I met her in all this time?" Kamone asked, reaching for his pack of cigarettes, and lighting them both one.

Lucci took several pulls from his cigarette before replying. "Because she's dead."

"I'm sorry," she apologized sincerely. "May I ask how she passed?"

Lucci rubbed his fingers over his eyes, trying to hide his tears as he took a deep breath. "David ... David killed her," he answered, almost in a whisper.

"What?" she gasped, sitting up. "What you mean, baby?"

Lucci took a long drag from his Newport allowing the ashes to fall in the water, staring blankly at the wall as if he were reliving the scene in his head.

"David was always jealous of me and mama's relationship as we were growing up," he began. "He always felt like mama loved me more than him, but that wasn't the case. She loved us both, but David was just born a bad seed. He was mannish, very destructive and mischievous. He stayed in some shit, and was always getting into trouble, whereas I was kinda shy. I loved school, and I loved to read. I stayed in all kinda school activities. Sports, plays, talent shows and mama loved it in me; I made her proud. I went to church with her every Sunday, and she even got me in the choir," he chuckled, remembering his first solo. "She knew I was going places in my life. I was gonna be something, somebody. And when mama found out that David was in a gang she sort of washed her hands of him. Tellin' him he would never be nothing but a thug. My father took care of us financially, but he was always too busy for his own family.

"At the time, he had just got his foot in the door of this big law firm, and he was more concerned with impressing them white muthafuckas who had they heels in his balls waiting for him to make one fuck up because he was the first nigga to be hired with their firm.

"So he never was around and all we had was mama. I admit, mama did throw me in David's face a lot. Tellin' him he should be like me, act more like me. But it was only because she loved him and she wanted him to leave them streets alone."

Tanika Lynch

Whore

Lucci lit up another cigarette and took a puff before continuing on. "One day, mama sent me down to the market to pick up some Gold Medal flour and a carton of eggs. I'll never forget that day. Us two were gonna make daddy this big pretty chocolate cake as a surprise, because he had won this huge publicized case. When I was coming back, I saw David on his knees in the middle of the street, screaming and crying, telling the neighbors that it was a mistake. I could feel it in my heart something was wrong with mama. I dropped them groceries and took off running to the house. It felt like I was wearing cement shoes. The faster I tried to run it seemed like the farther the house got. I couldn't get there fast enough. When I got inside I looked all over, screaming for mama. The last place I looked was mine and David's room. When I walked in ..." Lucci stopped as tears rolled down his face like a river. His hand shook violently as he put the cigarette up to his mouth, not realizing he was smoking the butt. "When I walked in," he started back up in a squeaky crackling voice as his chest heaved in and out, "Mama was layin' on the floor by David's bed with her dress pulled up to her stomach, her mouth and eyes open, her hand over her heart and lying in a pool of blood. David had shot her in the heart! I remember walkin' over to mama and pullin' down her dress, not wanting nobody to see her like that. I knew David had raped her cuz her panties were gone you know. And

mama wasn't the kind of woman to walk around without underpants on."

"It's OK, baby," Kamone said sympathetically, crying as well as she pried the cigarette butt from Lucci's hand, mad at herself for questioning his mother's death.

"After that, everything went black. The next thing I remember I was laying on the couch and police and paramedics were everywhere. I remember the stupid smirk on David's face as the police took him out in handcuffs. My father tried to attack David and three cops held him back as he cried like a baby asking David *why*? Why he would do something like that to his own mother? In court David's story was that mama was in our room snoopin' around and found a gun under his mattress. When she called him up and asked him about it he told her he was holding it for a friend. He said they got to arguing and mama talked about throwing it away. That's when he tried to grab it from her and it accidentally went off. I guess they didn't even check to see if she had been raped being that nobody would ever expect something like that. It never came up in court but I know he did it. He did it to defy her and to prove to her he was a man. I know how David thinks.

"But being that he was only 11, they sent him to a boys' home until he was 17 for manslaughter. I was mad at David for a long time but my mama came to me in a dream and told me to forgive him

Tanika Lynch

and I did. But daddy, he never forgave David. When they let him out of the home Daddy gave him two options. Either join the Marine Corps or die. So he joined the Marines.

"Somehow being that he served his country he got the charge expunged from his record. Then he joined the Police Academy. He became a police officer trying to make amends with Daddy. But Dad wants nothing to do with David. That why he wasn't at the party. He hates David. Everybody does. He's a lawless, scandalous bitch. I hit the streets out of guilt. Thinking that if I just woulda' been a troublemaker like David my mama would still be alive. That's why I say it's nothing left for us here. All I'll miss is visiting my mama's grave. But I know she still right here," he said, pointing to his heart.

"Yes she is, baby," Kamone agreed, seeing the sad little boy he had been the day his mother had died through his facial expressions. "And you're right." She placed Lucci's head on her chest and kissed his forehead. "There's isn't anything here for us."

Lucci had said it correct–nothing but bad memories were left in the city. Erasing their past and starting anew in another state was an excellent idea, especially since there might be a new addition to the family coming soon.

Kamone had planned to tell Lucci that she had missed her period while they were on their perfect

day out. But after that chaotic episode, her plans had been ruined. She decided that as soon as he got home from his trip she would surprise him with the good news.

Tanika Lynch

chapter
sixteen

Kamone smiled to herself as she stood at the kitchen sink doing the dishes, watching Paul and Ivory through the window as they played with a few of the neighborhood kids in the backyard.

Lucci had only been gone a few hours and she missed him already. She was bored with herself, and as it was the housekeeper's day off, she decided to do a little cleaning to keep her mind occupied.

Kamone was in the living room feeding the fish when the doorbell rang. She went to the door and looked through the peephole to find David on the porch holding two briefcases with a light-complected woman at his side.

She had been expecting him. Lucci left word that he would be dropping by with some drugs that he had illegally seized from another dealer after busting his house with a few of his sidekicks. She was to get the dope and put it in the safe in the

basement. That was it. She wasn't to allow him into the house for any reason. And she wasn't going to after hearing those horrifying stories about him last night.

She rolled her eyes and blew hot air from her mouth before opening the door.

"What's up, Ma?" He smiled, handing one of the briefcases to the woman. "We come with gifts."

"Hey how you doin'?" she asked dryly, reaching out for the briefcase.

"Hasn't Lucci taught you any manners?" he asked, removing his sunglasses. "Invite us in," he said as he pushed her to the side and barged in with his companion following behind. "Boy, I tell ya," he said as he walked into the living room, "you can take a bitch out the ghetto but not the ghetto out the bitch. Ain't that right, Maria?" he asked, looking back at the woman.

"Sí, Papi." Marie smiled, not bothering to pull down her short dress that rose up to her butt cheeks as she switched her way to the couch and plopped down.

"Lucci said you're not allowed in here if he's gone." Kamone frowned, standing her ground as she stood at the door.

"What?" David said, looking back at her as he sat the briefcase on the table. "You musta' heard him wrong." He flopped down onto the black mink couch. "My brotha' ain't said shit like that. Now, get over here. We got serious business ta tend to,"

Tanika Lynch

he ordered, patting a seat on the couch next to him.

"I already know the drill. We ain't got shit to discuss," she snapped, stomping over to the brief-case.

"Hold up, Ma," David said calmly, snatching the briefcase up and placing it on his lap. "Let's get one thang straight. I ain't Lucci, first off. So lower yo' tone when talkin' to me and watch yo' mouth before I kick it out. I'm runnin' this shit. And I'd advise you to follow orders—and get yo' ass over here before you find yo' self fucked up."

Kamone rolled her eyes yet kept her mouth shut, knowing David wasn't playing.

"Now, have a seat," he ordered.

Kamone slowly sat down as she looked over at Maria, who constantly smiled, chewed her gum and twirled her long, dyed blond hair around her finger as she sat with her legs wide open for David's pleasure on the couch across from them.

David popped open the case, exposing probably every drug known to man, in individual sandwich bags. "Let me see," he said, removing two healthy bags of white powder. "We'll need this, this and a lil' bit of this," he said, picking up a bag of mari-juana and some funny colored pills. He sat the items down on the table, closed up the case and placed it on the floor by his feet.

Kamone's hands began to sweat as she watched him pour a small mountain of each powered sub-stance onto the table. He pulled a box of cigars, a

razor and a crisp bill out of his pocket, and laid them onto the table. Her stomach began to twirl, already knowing he was up to no good.

David formed a crooked smile, looking back and forth at Kamone and Maria as he rolled the bill up as small as a cigarette, then held it up to his nose. He took a sniff of the one mountain, then went to the other. "Come here, baby," he said, beckoning Maria to come over as he wiped the excess powder from his nose.

Maria quickly jumped up, hurrying to get her nose dirty. David stroked her hair as she greedily sucked up the drugs, failing to come up for air.

"That's enough, you fuckin' Hoover!" David snapped, smacking the back of Maria's head. "Leave some for our pretty friend." He smiled, looking at Kamone.

"I don't do that," Kamone replied with authority in her tone.

"You mean, you don't do it no more?" David replied, grinning like the Grinch. "What, you forgot where you came from? You got the nerves to think you betta than somebody, huh?"

"I ... I think ya'll should go now. I gotta check on the kids," she said softly, trying to get up.

"Fuck them kids," he growled through tight lips as he grabbed the back of Kamone's neck and kept her seated. "You don't move unless I tell you to!" he said, shaking her back and forth. "A nigga can't even be nice to yo' ass. You like it gangsta, don't

Tanika Lynch

you? You want me to turn Ike Turner on yo' ass, huh?" he said, slamming her face down into the table. "Snort the dope, Anna Mae," he demanded, scrubbing her face into the powder.

Kamone struggled to breathe, waving her arms and kicking wildly as the powder got into her eyes, nose and mouth.

David grabbed the glock that he carried in his waistline and put it up to her head before raising her up. "Are you gonna be a good girl now?" he asked, pushing the nozzle of his gun deeper into her head.

"Da ... David, please!" she said, blinking her burning eyes rapidly as excess powder fell out of her mouth and nose. "Please, don't do this! The kids could come in at any minute. Please, I don't want them to see this!"

As if on cue, Kamone could hear the pitter patter of Ivory's feet as she ran laughing and screaming through the side door.

"Sister, sister," she laughed playfully through the kitchen, heading toward the living room. "Sister we ..." Ivory stopped and looked at Kamone as David placed the gun behind his back, looking curious and puzzled as she looked at the three. "Sister, you tricked me." She smiled. "I thought you said Lucci was gone to another state."

"Ivory, go back outside!" Kamone shouted, glad that she hadn't seen the gun.

"Are you and Lucci playing a game?" She

laughed and stepped closer. "Why you got that flour on you face, silly? You cookin' somethin'?"

"Ivory, I said go outside!" she shouted again with David's hand still around the back of her neck.

"Well, look what we got here." David smiled, pretending as if he were caressing Kamone's neck. "It's trick baby number one."

"My name not trick baby," she giggled. "It's piggy baby, 'member?"

"You sho' is pretty," he said, smiling at her as she stood in front of him. "You got pretty eyes to be so dark. And look at all that pretty curly hair," he said, reaching out to touch her curls.

"Take your ass outside!" Kamone screamed, freeing herself from David's grasp and pushing Ivory away.

"I just wanted some ice cream," Ivory pouted, not understanding what she did wrong.

"Take the whole box," Kamone replied, wiping the coke from her face. "And don't come back in here until I come get ya'll."

Ivory pouted with teary eyes as she folded her arms and turned around to stomp away. "Meanie flour face!" she shouted over her shoulder as she entered the kitchen, climbed onto a chair and got two boxes of popsicles before heading back outside, slamming the door behind her.

David laughed at the little girl's actions as he stood up into Kamone's face. "Unless you want that

Tanika Lynch

lil' trick baby to join the party I'd advise you to sit down and hear me out before I call curly Sue back in here."

Kamone flopped down onto the couch, close to tears, regretting even opening the front door.

"Now, this shit can go smooth and easy or it can get real rough up in here. The choice is yours. But one of three thangs is gonna happen today. And if you're smart you'll make the right choice."

Kamone looked over at Maria who was still holding the dollar bill, looking around as if nothing was even happening.

"I know everythang about you," he began. "You're a liar, a thief, a ho, a user and lets not forget a murderess bitch," he smirked, holding the gun to his side.

"What?" Kamone shouted, looking shocked. "Murder? I ain't neva' killed nobody!"

"Yeah right. You must really think that the shit you tell my brother is really a secret." He laughed. "Me and Lucci are much closer than he leads people to believe. And he tells me everythang. We keep nothing away from each other. And I do mean nothing," he emphasized, brushing the tip of his gun against her lips.

He turned away and walked off slowly. "I could just kill you like you killed that lady." He spun around and pointed his gun at Kamone, making both her and Maria jump in fear. "And of course I'll get away wit' it, being that I'm the law and all. I always come up with the best stories when I'm under pressure down at the station." He chuckled, turned back around and continued his walk throughout the living room.

"Or betta yet, I know some hoes who want yo' head. I could take you back down to yo' old stumpin' grounds, and watch them bitches tear you to pieces like vultures. Does the name Brittany ring a bell?" he asked, watching as Kamone squirmed in her seat at the name. "Or," he continued, "I could just put you under arrest for murder, kidnapping and possession of narcotics." He waved his hands over the drug-filled table. "And some more shit I can think up on the way downtown. Then I'll get my partnas to pop Lucci's stupid ass for harboring a fugitive, accessory after the fact, statutory rape and we'll bust every joint he owns. Now you may not care about yourself but I know you don't wanna be Lucci's downfall after he's been so damn good to you. So, breathe easy and make the right choice."

"What's the right choice?" she asked, already knowing that it wasn't any better that the last two choices he gave her.

"Number three," he said with a smirk, putting his gun away. "We can forget about all the other shit, sit back, get blowed and then I'ma tear that pussy up and show you what you missin' out on since you chose Lucci over me. That's all a nigga want, Ma. Lucci told me all about that killa head you workin' wit. Not to mention that hypnotic ass,"

Tanika Lynch

he lied. "Give me what I want and everybody can continue on with happy lives. Lucci will never find out, unless you tell him," he said, popping two pills in his mouth.

Kamone's lip quivered as she held back her tears, refusing to let him see her cry. She didn't have much of a choice in the matter. She knew that if David could do what he did to his own mother he would surely follow through with everything he said on her and his own brother.

"Why you want me so bad?" Kamone asked in a shivering voice. "You talked about me like a dog and now you want me?"

David took a seat back on the couch between the two women before replying.

"Whatever David wants David gets. That's all the explanation I can give you! That and the fact that Lucci holding you hostage from the world like yo' shit golden. That makes me want you even more. I don't like being deprived of nothing."

"You said nobody will know, but what about her?" Kamone asked, looking at Maria.

"She can't understand shit we sayin'." David laughed. "And she only speaks Spanish. Watch this," he said, turning to Maria. "Would you like a shit sandwich, bitch?" he asked her with a friendly smile.

"Sí, Papi," Maria answered as she stared at the drugs, waiting for permission to snort.

"Now, fuck all these games," he began, handing

the rolled up bill to Kamone. "Let's get down to business. You can do this yourself, or I can force feed it to you. Go ahead and take a nose dive. You know you missed this shit."

Kamone hesitantly took the bill from his hand, closing her eyes tight as she lowered herself into the powder. Being that she had been clean for a good while, she got an instant rush. Her nose was burning, her head was spinning and her heart began beating fast. A single tear dropped from her eyes from the hurt, shame and guilt she felt all through her body.

She was hurt because she had no control over her own life. Time and time again, people had always forced her into doing what they wanted her to do, by blackmailing her with the devoted, unconditional love that she openly displayed for the people closest to her. She was ashamed because even though drugs had helped to destroy her life at one point in time, she had always enjoyed the feeling it gave her. And how could she allow herself to feel so good at such a time?

Her guilt came from the fact that she felt all this was her fault. If she didn't come into Lucci's life, David wouldn't be threatening to destroy him because of her. She knew Lucci would be heartbroken if he ever found out about this. But he would be even more hurt if he came home to a tragedy that she could have prevented. The last thing she wanted to do was hinder and hurt the man who had

Tanika Lynch

been through the storm with her. She would just give David what he wanted so he could go away and then everything would be over, at least she thought.

After almost an hour of getting high, and David saw that Kamone was now in a different state of mind, he opened up his second suitcase and pulled out various sex toys, dildos and a video camera.

Kamone sat fighting to keep her eyes open. Seeing everything in 3-D, David had her snorting both cocaine and blow without her knowledge, giving her body an up and down effect.

All Kamone could remember was David stripping her of her clothes as she sat paralyzed on the couch. She went into deep nods as David and Maria took turns having sex with her. Yet, David only video taped when she and Maria were going at it.

For several days straight, David came over with different women to repeat the act over and over again, secretly giving her an addiction to heroin and an unwanted taste of the lesbian world, as he video taped it all.

David led her to believe that everything would stop when Lucci came back home, but the Devil, David, was a liar who came to steal, kill and destroy!

Just when Kamone thought the rain was over in her life, and she was now seeing the sunshine, the biggest storm ever was headed her way.

Triple Crown Publications presents . . .

Tanika Lynch

chapter
seventeen

Lucci sat at the red light smiling like a kid on Christmas as he took another look at the exquisite platinum and diamond ring that he picked up for Kamone while in California. While he was there he not only found the perfect land to have their dream house built on but also the perfect engagement ring to ask for Kamone's hand in marriage.

He couldn't wait to get home to his family but he really couldn't wait to see the look on Kamone's face when he asked her to be his wife. He wanted to do it today but he also wanted it to be a moment they could both remember years from now. So, he was going to wait until he came up with the perfect plan.

He already had it all mapped out. He was going to get in touch with his father and find out how he could legally marry her being that she was still a minor and had no parents to sign a consent form. Then he would take the necessary steps to adopt

Paul and Ivory to make their family complete. Even if he had to wait until she reached 18, he would. But nothing was going to stop him from being with her until the casket dropped.

Maybe it was just him, but today was the loveliest summer day ever. The weather wasn't too hot, the air smelled fresh and the birds seemed to be chirping in a harmonious melody. The only thing that worried him was the fact that he hadn't been able to reach Kamone since he had been gone. Every time he called, the phone just rang. He made himself think that she was probably just in and out the house with the kids, which made her miss his calls. But on the other hand, not knowing what was going on with her made him uneasy. So being that his business had been taken care of earlier than he expected, he decided to come back home a day earlier. He couldn't stand the thought of being away from Kamone and the kids another day.

As he headed home he picked up his cellular to call David. They had some unfinished business on the table and he wanted to let David know that he was back home and would be dropping by later on to discuss it.

When he called David's home he didn't pick up. So he hit him on his cellular knowing that David carried it with him at all times.

"What's up, bro?" Lucci said into the phone, sounding extra happy.

"What's crackin', big fella," David replied on his

way over to see Kamone while still on duty.

"How's the weather down there in Cali?"

"It was sweet but I ain't there no more. I just got back in Detroit 'bout an hour ago and I'm headed to the crib."

Damn! David thought to himself, making a U-turn to head home, mad that his plans had been ruined.

"My business got taken care of early. So I decided to come on back home. Ain't shit down there for me."

"I hear you man," David said, speeding down the streets. "How 'bout you stop by my place before you go home?"

"I called to tell you I'll be through tonight to handle that business we discussed. But right now I'm tired as hell. I got jet lag like a mug," he explained, rubbing his tired eyes.

"Naw, dog. I gotta pull a double," he lied. "You need to come see me like right now. I'm on my way home. This is important, all bullshit aside."

Lucci exhaled as he checked his watch. "All right, man. I'll be there in about 10 minutes."

"I'll be waiting," David replied before hanging up his phone.

Lucci threw his phone into the passengers seat, wondering what in the world David had to tell him that was so important. He just hoped it wasn't a waste of his time. He had to get home to surprise his family.

When Lucci drove up, David was standing on his front porch, smoking a blunt with his uniform on. David shook his head in pity, giving Lucci a sad look as he approached.

"What's up, man?" Lucci asked, seeing the messed-up expression on David's face as he gave him a hand pound.

"Babyboy," David said, taking Lucci into the house. "I love you, and no matter what differences we have, you still my brother. I got your best interest at heart. There's no nice way to put this," he said, walking into the living room and grabbing a DVD from his collection. "So I'ma just say it flat out. Yo' girl ain't to be trusted."

"Go'n with that noise, man," Lucci said, smacking his lips and flapping his hand at David. "You can't tell me ..."

"Just hear me out," David interrupted, popping the DVD into the player. "I know how you are, and when my street sources told me that some chicks they know was goin' around talkin' about how they had been trickin' with Lucci's girl, and she was gettin' them high and givin' them money, I didn't believe it myself. I told them niggas I'd pay them a grip if they gave me some hardcore proof, because I knew you wouldn't just take my word on it."

"Fuck yo' street resources," Lucci growled. "Ain't no way in the fuck my woman givin' nobody my dope and money—all right! And you's a sick man for even tryin' to convince me she a dyke!

Tanika Lynch

That ain't even possible!"

Just as Lucci said those words David pushed play, placing the volume on mute so Lucci couldn't hear his voice instructing Kamone on what to do as he recorded it. Lucci's mouth dropped open and his heart sank into his spine as the sight of Kamone on her knees licking another woman's vagina filled the screen. He was close to tears as he watched Kamone, who looked intoxicated by the eyes, as she dipped her finger into the cocaine that lay in a black tray on the nightstand and sniffed it before dipping again and rubbing it all over her vagina. She then assumed the doggy style position and allowed the unknown woman to lick it clean.

"I know it hurts," David said, walking over to Lucci and placing his hand onto his shoulder con-solingly. "But it's better you found out from me instead of gettin' embarrassed in the streets. That bitch gonna be yo' downfall, man. Get rid of her."

"Get yo' hands off me!" Lucci frowned, knocking David's hand away as he turned to leave. He knew that David was loving every minute of his pain. And he didn't show him the tape out of love and concern but to rub the fact that he was right in his face.

"What's I do?" David smirked, cracking up as Lucci slammed the door in his face. His plan had worked. Lucci fell for it and was hurt to the pits of his soul. Now if everything else fell into place like he hoped, pretty ass would be all his before the day

was out.

Lucci drove through traffic like a maniac as tears of anger flowed from his eyes. He ran red lights hurrying home as visions of that tape ran through his mind.

He really didn't want to believe that Kamone, of all people, would play him like that after all they'd been through. He knew before he left that she was falling down because of the incident with her mother, and he feared that she might relapse like ex-addicts sometimes did after suffering trauma. Now his worst fear was dead in his face! But to top it all off, she wasn't turning tricks. She was the trick, and with other females at that, which was believable and to be expected since she had been gang raped.

He couldn't believe how the manipulative bitch had played with his heart and mind. He trusted her with his life and told her all his darkest secrets. And all along she had been wearing a mask.

His sick mind kicked in and he began to think about all the times he left her alone with his unweighed dope and the maid. There was no telling how long she had been betraying him, waiting on the right time to clean him out and disappear like she was known to do.

He was hurt and his mind was in another place. All he ever asked her to do was keep it real with him. He loved her so much that he would have been willing to work out whatever she was going

Tanika Lynch

through, with her. But now it was too late. She had humiliated him, stole from him, and most importantly, she had betrayed and lied to him. Lucci was big on loyalty, and he wanted nothing to do with a bitch he couldn't trust!

He came to a screeching halt, parking sideways in front of his house. He was so heated that he jumped out, leaving the car running and the driver's door wide open.

His hands shook as he keyed open the door. His blood was beyond boiling and sweat ran from the crown of his head onto his neck. When he walked into the house, Kamone was on the couch in a deep nod with drugs laid out on the table. Her body had developed the need for smack since David had fed it to her for six days straight. She woke up that morning needing it just to get out of bed.

Lucci's eyes popped at the sight of her looking like a common junkie with drugs laid out where the kids could get to them, and he just snapped.

He howled like a vicious wolf as he ran and kicked over the table before snatching Kamone up.

"Baby, why?" he cried, throwing her across the room into a wall. "Bitch, why would you do this to us?" he screamed, stomping over to her as she lay there with dreary eyes, thinking she was hallucinating. "I trusted you!" He picked her up and slapped her right back down. "I loved you! Even when they told me I was crazy for fuckin' with you I gave you a chance," he said, picking her up again

and body slamming her on the couch. "I found you in the trash and turned you into a queen. And this is how you play me?"

Kamone quickly came to her senses as Lucci straddled her and smacked her again. "Baby, wait!" she cried, shielding her face as blood ran from her nose and lip. "Lucci, please listen to me baby! I ..."

"Ain't no explaining! I seen it for myself!" Lucci wrapped his hands around her neck and choked her. "You made a fool of me! You fucked up our life—all for some drugs. They was right about you! You'll never change! You'll always be a worthless fiended-out bitch just like yo' mama!"

Kamone scratched at his arms as her eyes dilated, her ears popped and she felt herself becoming weak from the lack of oxygen.

"Lucci, stop!" Ivory screamed, awakened by all the noise. "Get off her!" she cried, windmilling Lucci's arms and back.

"Get off her!" Paul shouted, running behind Ivory and punching at Lucci's feet.

"You gettin' outta my house, bitch!" he said, ignoring the kids as he stood up and dragged Kamone by the hair like a caveman all the way to the front door.

Paul and Ivory followed behind, crying and screaming for Lucci to stop, as they held on to Kamone's legs, being dragged as well.

"Lucci!" she cried, choking as she heaved for air. "It's not what you think! It's not what you

Tanika Lynch

think! Just listen to me!" she said, grabbing onto the wall and legs of chairs to prevent him from putting her out.

Lucci ignored her as he got to the door and wrestled to get Paul and Ivory off her legs. He then picked her up by the waist, opened the door, carried her out kicking and screaming and threw her face down onto the front lawn as Ivory and Paul stood sobbing and throwing tantrums.

"Get the fuck on, bitch!" he yelled as he turned his back to her and walked toward the porch.

"Lucci," she sobbed, lying on her stomach and reaching out to him. "Baby, please don't do me like this! I need you! You just don't understand!"

"Oh, I understand all right," he said, picking up the kids as they swung wildly at him. "You the one that needs to understand. Understand that you fucked up the best thang that coulda eva happen to yo' poor ass! Understand that you's a pitiful deceitful bitch! Understand that you don't need me, you need God! He's the only one that can help a worthless bitch like you!" he said, turning to step into the house. "You'll never see me or these kids again! A bitch like you don't deserve people like us!"

"But, Lucci, I'm carrying your baby!" she whined, slobbing at the mouth as she stood to her feet and held her belly.

Lucci stopped in his tracks as if he had been hit by a Mac truck. He placed the kids down into the house, before turning around slowly to face her.

"You just don't quit do you?" he said, quivering in the voice. "Why would you hurt me of all people? Why me? You's a lying bitch. You'll say anything to get your way. And just to think ..." he said, shaking his head as tears rolled from his swollen eyes, "I was gonna make you my wife. Get the fuck off my property!" he yelled, wiping his face. "Go where the fuck you belong before I call the police on you and get yo' young ass locked up for life!" he threatened, watching as she ran barefooted away from the house. Lucci looked around grimly as all his nosey neighbors stood on their porches, watching the show.

In the other direction David sat in his patrol car watching the show as well. He got there just in time to see Lucci throwing Kamone out on her ass.

He knew that Kamone was all messed up and bitter with sweet ole Lucci at this point in time. And now it was his turn to be the good guy.

Tanika Lynch

chapter
eighteen

David drove slowly behind Kamone as she ran for blocks away from Lucci's house. She stopped to release the vomit that was brewing in her stomach, not knowing whether it was the dope, stress or morning sickness that made her hurl her guts out right in front of someone's driveway.

"Ah," David called out, watching her wipe her mouth as she stood bent over, holding her stomach. "You all right, Ma?" he asked, trying to sound worried.

When Kamone turned around and saw David's face, she threw up again. "Leave me the fuck alone!" she cried, spitting out left-over vomit and wiping her mouth with the sleeve of her pajama top. "You got what you wanted, you twisted bastard! Now just leave me alone!" she screamed, speeding up her pace.

"What?" David replied, playing dumb as he drove alongside her. "What you talkin' 'bout? I was

just on my way over to see you when I saw you running from the house and Lucci standing on the porch. What was that about?"

"You know what it was about, dirty bastard! You told him. You told him what's been going on!" she cried, walking even faster.

"What? I ain't even seen Lucci, girl. I didn't even know he was back in town," David replied, trying to sound upset. "I just wanted to have fun with you. I didn't have a reason to tell. You sure it wasn't that big mouth-ass housekeeper? She seen me leave once. I mean, what did he say to you?"

Kamone walked in silence, replaying the incident. Lucci really hadn't said much of anything. He just came in swinging and calling her out her name. Then she remembered that she had dope laying on the table because she hadn't been expecting him. Maybe his anger stemmed from that. But still, David had been the one who started her back to using. All this shit was still his fault.

"Why don't you get in and talk to me, Kamone? You out here barefooted and shit all in yo' pajamas. Come on, get in and let's talk about this," he suggested, stopping his car and getting out.

"I ain't going nowhere with you!" she screamed as she took off running.

"Kamone!" he yelled, running behind her. "Come here. It's not what you think! I'm sorry!"

Some of the residents watched in awe at the officer running after the barefooted, bloody-faced young girl, wondering what she had done. They whispered amongst themselves as the officer caught the girl, threw her against a car and hand-cuffed her as she screamed bloody murder.

"Everything's OK, folks," David said, smiling as he threw Kamone over his shoulder and carried her back to the patrol car.

"He's a killer!" she screamed, kicking and jerk-ing, trying to get away. "He's trying to kill me!" she declared, hoping someone would help.

"She's on drugs, people," David explained to the gawking viewers as he sprinted back to his patrol car and threw her into the back seat before speeding off.

"Kamone, please listen to me," he yelled over her screams. "I'm sorry for the shit I did to you. But you gotta understand it's not really my fault."

"Take these handcuffs off me!" she screamed, kicking the wired window that separated the front and back seat.

"If you calm down and listen to me, I will! I'm not gonna hurt you, all right? I just need you to hear me out."

Kamone exhaled as she put her feet on the floor, feeling dizzy and exhausted from all she had been through. "Listen to you for what? What the fuck can you tell me?" she said in anger.

"I know I been foul to you, all right? I know that. And I'm sorry. Don't nobody understand like me. All my life everybody always looked down on me.

Making me be the dogmatic-ass nigga I am today. I don't wanna be like that. I'm a human, and I got feelings, too."

"What the fuck all that got to do with me?" she shouted. "Why would you do this to me? I ain't never did shit to you!"

"Kamone ... I got problems. I don't know ... just can't ... I can't keep going through this shit!" he yelled, pounding on his steering wheel. "I need help. I just need somebody to talk to. I gotta get this shit off my chest. I ain't never felt so dead in my life," he said, stopping his car on a side street and covering his eyes up with his hands, as if he were crying. "I swear on my life, I didn't want to hurt you like that. I don't wanna see you out here like this. I know it's my fault. Everything's all my fault. I can't even do my fuckin' job without thinkin' about you. Just please, please listen to me. Let me just explain my side of the story."

Kamone sat looking at David, not even knowing he could be so emotional. He sounded so sincere, and she may as well listen to what he had to say. She had nothing to lose from it; everything was messed up anyways. She didn't even care if he killed her. Right about now, she wanted to die anyways.

"Will you take these things off me first?" she asked softly, letting down her guard a little.

David looked back at her, wiping away the spit he had placed under his eyes to make it appear as

Tanika Lynch

if he were crying. "OK," he agreed, stepping out the car, taking her out the back seat and putting her into the front before removing them. "Here," he said, taking a cigarette from his pack and lighting it before handing it to her, then lighting himself one. "Kamone," he began, blowing smoke from his nose, "you just can't even began to imagine the real. You still young and very naive. You been blinded and don't even realize it."

"What you mean, blinded?" she asked, shaking as she placed the cigarette up to her busted lip.

"Nothin'. Just forget about it, Ma. You wouldn't believe me anyways," he said, turning to look out his window. "I mean, I wouldn't even expect you to. I know you gotta be thinkin' the worst of me right now. And I feel fucked up even playing a part of this shit. I'm getting too old for these kinda games."

"What you talkin' about?" she asked, hot boxing her cigarette.

"If I tell you," he began, turning to face her, "will you not hold this shit against me?"

"I can't promise you nothin'. How could you even ask me that after what you've done to me?"

"I know that. And like you said, you haven't done anything to me. That's why I feel you need to know what's really goin' on," he said, working hard on Kamone's vulnerability. He had her right where he wanted her. Now, all he had to do was turn her against Lucci, and get her mind focused on him.

"What do I need to know?" she asked, looking at him curiously. "Just say what you gotta say."

David drove on in silence for a moment, thinking his lies through thoroughly before speaking.

"Everybody got me labeled as the bad nigga, the heartless monster. But Lucci is a heartless monster in his own way, Ma. He plays that sensitive shit because it gets him his way. He's a confused man. He don't know what he wants. But he's still my brother, and I love him."

"What are you talkin' about? Stop ramblin' and get to the point!" she demanded.

"There's no easy way to put it," he started, throwing his cigarette out the window. "So I'ma just say it. Lucci is sweet meat ... a butt fucker. A nigga livin' on the D.L. He wasn't in Cali on business. He was in Cali romancin' his man."

"What?" she yelped. "Yeah, right! I don't believe that!"

"You don't gotta believe me, Ma. The proof is in the puddin'. Don't get me wrong, he likes pussy a lil' bit, but dick is his first love. Always has been. He's a Rick James type of nigga. Loves em' and leave em'. Ya'll like dolls to him. He plays with you for a while, and when he get tired of ya'll he makes me do the dirty work and get ya'll outta his hair. He gotta long distance relationship with this kat that goes to college in California. Some Pretty Ricky-ass nigga. They got some kinda understandin' that Lucci can play while he's away, but only with

Tanika Lynch

women. That way, he wouldn't lose him. Well the nigga about to graduate, and he's on his way home to Lucci. That's why you got booted. His man gave him orders to clean house. Remember when I told you that we was closer than he leads you to believe? I wasn't lying. Yeah, we got our problems but we play the distances game to keep people guessin'. Lucci gave me the whole run down on you, Ma. And he put me up to the shit I did to you. Now I feel bad about it."

"Lucci loves me. Why would he do something like that to me?" she whimpered, trying to make sense of the story.

"That was the problem. He did kinda fall in love with you. I guess you weren't like the other women or something because he told his man how he was feelin' and they had this big fallin' out. Ole boy was steaming.

"He been with Lucci for five years now. Then Lucci sorta came to his senses, and he told ole boy he would do anythang to make it up to him. And from my understanding, Ole boy hates yo' guts for almost stealin' his man away. And he told Lucci if he really loved him he would put you back the way he found you. The only reason why he kept them kids was cuz him and ole boy always talked about adoptin' kids and raisin' a family together. I guess you was just the right sucka that came along at the wrong time.

"Lucci gave me orders to handle you. He told

me what he wanted done and being that I was a little jealous that you chose him over me I went along with it. But along the way I grew feelins for you. And I didn't have no intentions on tellin' him nothin'. Like I said. I didn't even know he was back. I guess he figured the plan was in motion so he came through the door trippin' cuz he already knew what was crackin'."

Kamone sat crying to herself, putting it all together. Even though David wasn't the most trustworthy person it didn't take a wizard to see that what he was saying was the truth. She thought about how he had no woman in his life when they first met. And fine as he was, there were no signs of a woman ever existing in his life or home. The only people who called the house were his so-called partners. Her sick mind kicked in, and she thought about how Lucci had turned her down when she came on to him. Using her age as an excuse. And then, she had to cry, beg and plead for him to have sex with her. All that sensitive shit was just the sissy in him. And David was right, she was back to the way he had found her. Broke, beat up, barefooted and addicted! But what really got under her collar was the fact that Lucci had stolen her brother and sister to raise with his faggot-ass man! She hated Lucci's guts. She didn't care if she never saw him again, but she'd be damned if he thought for one minute she would just up and leave Ivory and Paul without making any noise.

Tanika Lynch

Whore

"Don't cry, Ma," David said softly, rubbing her thigh consolingly. "A nigga like Lucci don't deserve a woman like you anyways. And being that I was wrong as hell, I wanna make it up to you anyway I can."

"How 'bout helping me get my brother and sister back," she huffed, wiping her face.

"All that will come, but right now, you gotta worry 'bout you. Lucci ain't gonna hurt em' or nothin' like that. They safe for now. So how 'bout I take you to my house, and you take a hot bath, have a drink, or whatever else you wanna do, and relax until I come back from work. Then we can talk about all this. I promise you, I won't make you do nothin' you don't wanna do. I just wanna help you, Ma. That's the only motive I got right now."

Kamone studied him for a moment, already knowing that she had nothing to lose from this point on. She was homeless, pregnant and worst of all, she had a habit that she couldn't support without help. And since David wanted so badly to help her, she was going to accept it by all means. At this point, she felt just as heartless as David, and being that he was so out cold, she planned to use him to get back at everybody who had ever fucked her over! She was coming at all her enemies with a vengeance. And whatever she had to do to convince this sick bastard David into being her tool would be done!

Triple Crown Publications presents . . .

Tanika Lynch

chapter
nineteen

Kamone's body began to twitch at the sight of the heroin that David poured onto the long slab of glass that lay on the den table. David had left her high and dry all day and she was in desperate need of the dope.

She had been living with him for almost a week now and his small two bedroom brick house was nothing like Lucci's mini-mansion. Even though he had a good job and did a lot of illegal stuff, it was obvious he didn't spend his money on nice things for his home. Dishes were piled to the rim in his kitchen sink and other than beer and liquor, there were only a few items in his refrigerator. He had a permanent piss stain around his toilet, dirty clothes lay all around the house, fast food wrappers and junk food filled his trash and his old navy blue leather furniture was damaged with smokers' holes and reeked of spilled liquor. He was a slob and the junkie in him showed in the way he lived. Yet

Kamone couldn't complain as she once lived in worse. Besides, she had no place else to go and David wasn't as bad as she thought he would be.

"Why them dishes still in that sink?" he asked, taking his slow time opening the bag of cocaine and placing it along side the blow.

"Um ... I been sick, David," Kamone answered looking at the drugs like a fat kid staring through the window of a bakery. "I been sittin' right here on this couch waitin' on you to come back. It seems like you were gone forever."

"I gotta do my job, Ma." He chuckled, then slowly scooped a wad of the coke up with the long fingernail on his pinkey, placing it up to his nose and watching Kamone lick her lips as he sopped up every last drop. "Damn, that's some good shit," he teased, knowing Kamone was fiending.

"I been sick all day," she repeated, scratching her arm and becoming irritated in her seat. "I think it's the stress," she added, unwilling to admit her hunger for the dope.

"You know the best part of being a cop?" David pushed the glass toward her. "You ain't neva' gotta waste yo' money on dope. You can just run up on a nigga and take his shit." He laughed. "Them niggaz hate sittin' in the county in the midst of summer."

He loosened the top button of his uniform shirt, rubbing Kamone's bare leg as he watched her go back and forth between the two piles, sucking the powder up like juice. "Don't hurt yo' self, Ma." He smiled, hoping that as soon as the blow gave her the fix she needed and the coke boosted her system, she would be all over him like melting butter on mashed potatoes.

Kamone flung her head up, tilting it all the way back onto the couch, savoring the tingling sensation that the drugs gave her. It felt like a thousand feathers lightly stroking her skin from the inside out.

"You feel good, don't you?" he asked in a low seductive voice, reaching out to touch her nipples that stuck out like eraser heads on a number two pencil through the white T-shirt he had given her to wear.

"David, stop," she slurred, removing his hand in a delayed reaction, looking at him through sedated eyes.

"What's the matter, baby? I came home on duty just to hook you up and get a lil' ass before I hit the streets again," he replied, lunging over at her and kissing her roughly. "Come on baby, let me hit it right fast. I got my partner waitin' in the car and shit."

"David, stop!" she shouted, pushing him away. "I had that dream again, and you promised me you wouldn't make me do anything I didn't want to. I don't wanna do nothin' when I have those dreams."

"Damn, girl!" he frowned, jumping off the couch and readjusting his hard penis through his

pants. "My dick rock hard, and you keep talkin' like Martin Luther King!"

"I already told you I can't stop having them dreams until I face my fears. I gotta get that bitch Brittany. That's the only way I can get it out my head," she explained, looking up at him with a spellbinding look in her heavenly eyes that entranced the male race. "David, I want you just as bad as you want me, baby. But everytime I have that dream, I feel like I'm being raped all over again. You know what I've been though, and I'll never be right as long as Brittany still breathing." She stood in front of him and threw back her curly, wet hair as she bit down on her bottom lip innocently. "You just don't know how bad I want her head. She destroyed me! She destroyed my life."

"I understand all that, but I got needs. You been layin' up dick teasin' me, knowing how bad I want that ass. I mean, damn, don't you think a nigga deserve somethin'? I done took you in, put a roof over yo' head, feed you and yo' habit. I got feelings for you," he said, grabbing her up like a brute and squeezing her behind. "You my woman now, and it's time we consummate our relationship."

"I know, baby, but I wouldn't be able to give you my all with this shit weighing on my mind like this. When we lay down I wanna concentrate on only you. I gotta get it all outta my mind. It's driving me crazy, and I'm so worried my brother and sister. Lucci might be hurting Paul or something."

Tanika Lynch

Whore

Big crocodile tears rolled down her cheeks as she laid her head on his chest.

David's nose flared as he bit the sides of his jaws deep in thought. He was tired of being nice about this shit but he really did like Kamone and he wanted her to love him just as much as she had loved his brother.

He kissed the top of her head before pushing her away, picking up the glass slab and taking a few sniffs of cocaine. "When I come back," he began, buttoning his shirt back up, "have those dishes done and be ready for me." He turned around and looked at her once more before leaving without saying another word.

When Kamone heard the door slam shut, she smiled wickedly with malicious thoughts running through her brain. She had been planting seeds in David's head since day one. Trying to manipulate him into playing captain save-a-ho. She deprived him of sex, telling him flashbacks of her rape had been flickering through her mind, leaving her depressed and afraid of being touched. She knew David hated to be deprived and she hoped it would give him the idea to take care of the problem that was keeping him from getting what he wanted so badly. She didn't understand why David had such a strong urge to obtain her love and acceptance but she was going to play on it while she could.

She wanted Brittany first because she felt it was her fault that her luck in life was so bad. If it

weren't for Brittany, she wouldn't have gone to that dopespot and gotten raped. She wouldn't have met Lucci, killed Cookie or be in the situation she was in now.

After Brittany was taken care of, her next target was Lucci. She planned on having David to strip him of everything he owned then throw him in jail so she could get Paul and Ivory back. After that she would knock off David by poisoning his dope and watch him die a slow death. He thought she was naive and had forgiven him for what he had done but he wasn't off the hook. She just needed him to clear the coast and make the way for her to get to where she wanted to be. After she did him in she would take all the money and dope he had seized from Lucci and disappear into thin air with Paul, Ivory and the baby she was carrying.

She planned to have all this done before she began to show. She had no intentions of getting rid of her baby regardless of how Lucci had played her. Even though she hated him now, she had loved him to no ends when they created their child.

This child would remind her of the strongest love she probably would never feel again from a man, and also mark the start of a new life. She planned to stop using just as soon as her mission was complete. She knew it wasn't good for the baby, but she wasn't really worried, being that her mother did drugs with her and Ivory, and they came out perfectly normal. She was going to move

Tanika Lynch

far away and give Paul, Ivory and her unborn child the life they deserved.

She had it all figured out. She just prayed it all worked out.

It was almost one in the morning when David came staggering into the house with a bottle of Moet in one hand and a big black leather purse in the other.

He stumbled into the den where Kamone still sat nodding out from indulging herself with the drugs he had left for her.

He flopped down beside her, grabbed her face and woke her up by tongue kissing her passionately.

Kamone frowned, tasting his liquored-up breath as she became alert. "Gone," she replied, leaning away from him.

"Will you love me, Ma?" David asked, dragging his words. "I want you to love me. I want you to be proud of me," he said, gazing into her eyes.

"I already told you..."

"Shhh," he whispered, putting his finger to his lips. "It might hear you."

"What? Who might hear me?" she asked, looking puzzled as she looked behind him, thinking he brought company home.

"I don't know what it is about you," he said, removing a pair of black leather police gloves from his back pocket, "but you got my mind. You done hexed me or somethin'."

Kamone watched him suspiciously as he unzipped the purse while mumbling jibberish.

"I think this might be the craziest shit I've ever done," he said, reaching inside with both hands, "but your wish is my command," he chuckled, bringing out Brittany's extremely swollen, bloody head. There were holes where her eyes once were and something that looked like a wrinkled Tootsie Roll stick with veins hanging from the ends had been stuffed into her mouth.

Kamone's high was instantly blown as she scrambled to get off the couch and fell to the floor. She let out a blood curdling scream as she crawled like a baby to a far corner. "What the fuck's wrong with you?" she cried, shielding herself against the wall as she stared at him and the head with frightened eyes and her heart pounding like a beating drum.

"It's what you wanted," he replied, cocking his head and looking at his work. "You wanted the bitch's head ... here it is. It wasn't an easy task neither. I had to find the bitch, arrest her for sellin' ass and then drive her all the way to Belle Isle. I had to whoop the nigga's ass and drag the faggot all the way to the wooded area. I tied her to this tree and the first thang I did was dig them eyeballs out. I stuck em' in that open ass of hers," he explained, making a face as if he could still smell the funk, "so she could see what it felt like to be violated. She wouldn't stop screamin' so I cut her dick off and

Tanika Lynch

stuffed it in her mouth. Then I stood there talkin' to her about what she did to you until she took her last breath. I got her, baby." He snickered. "Now you can stop having those dreams," he said, dropping the head back in the purse. "She had a nice purse." He took off the gloves and put them into the purse also. "I thought you might like it." He smiled, then zipped the purse up and threw it to the floor. "I did what you wanted me to do," he said, wiping his soaking wet, sweaty face before quickly removing the mud and blood-stained uniform. "Now it's time for you to hold up yo' end."

Kamone rocked back and forth, her arms wrapped around her legs. She cried and whimpered softly. Suddenly, David walked over to her butt-naked with his long hard penis held firmly in his hand.

"David ... nooo," she whined in a low tone, not wanting him to touch her after committing such a brutal act.

David leaned down and picked her up as if she weighed nothing, placing her back against the wall as he rammed himself inside her, pounding her as hard as he could as he grunted like a savage beast.

Kamone lay limp, looking like a rag doll as David enjoyed himself. Her eyes were glued on the purse that lay only inches away. She couldn't believe that David actually did something like that. She wanted Brittany dead, but she didn't want to witness the grotesque act. David was really a sick

man and she realized that using him to do her dirt wouldn't come without penalty.

She didn't realize that David was drawn to her for his own twisted reasons and because of this, he would do anything she asked of him in return for her acceptance. He would take out anyone who got in the way of their love—even her.

Tanika Lynch

chapter
twenty

Kamone hung her head low in humiliation as a group of girls her age passed by, criticizing her appearance and giggling in her face.

"Ewww, look at her," one of the girls said brazenly.

Kamone just ignored them. She had gone to the convenience store that was just a few blocks over to pick up a few things. Being that she had no clothes of her own she put on one of David's sweat suits that just swallowed her up and a pair of his size 12 Nike flip-flops on her size 7 feet. She had winged herself for blow after experiencing an overdose scare and it showed physically.

Her hair, which once had a natural shine, was now dull and broken off. Her skin appeared dry and ashen and her eyes were similar to that of a raccoon. She looked just like she felt and the bad part about it was that she didn't really care.

While she was out she noticed that there was a

church not too far from David's house. She wouldn't have paid it any attention had it not been for the big pretty sign outside which told the name of the church. She realized that it was the church that Mr. Roberts had invited her to. She knew that with tomorrow being Sunday Mr. Roberts would probably be there, but she had no intention on going. She was too ashamed of herself and she didn't feel worthy enough to step in the house of the God he had told her about.

She picked up her pace, hurrying home to clean the house. As she had kicked off the drugs for a little over a week, the house looked even more of a mess since she hadn't been able to do anything but lay in bed. She planned to give the house the best cleaning it probably ever had. Then she would take a nice hot bath before David came home from work. She knew it would make her feel much better, and allow her to get her thoughts in order.

When she got to the house, the first thing she did was crank up the stereo. Music always put her in a joyous mood and motivated her to do things she really didn't feel like doing.

She began cleaning in the living room and worked her way up to the bedroom. She could tell David hadn't cleaned in years by the many cobwebs that occupied various corners of the house and the thick dust and dirt that she collected on her cleaning rag.

When she got to the bedroom, she began to

Tanika Lynch

rearrange David's bedroom furniture, trying to make the cluttered area seem more organized and spacious.

She was moving his dresser when she noticed that a cocoa brown-colored photo album had been hidden on the floor behind it. She picked it up and opened it without a second thought to feed her curiosity.

On the very first page was an old Polaroid picture of David and Lucci as toddlers. They looked so cute in their matching outfits and baseball caps. They even had the same wide smile that showed off their identical set of dimples.

She flipped through the album, smiling and laughing at different photos of them growing up. When she got to one particular photo, she almost dropped the book. Her jaw dropped as she stared at the photo of Lucci and David, who appeared to be no older than three or four, as they sat on the lap of a woman who could have passed for Kamone's identical twin. If another person had been looking at the photos with her they would bet a million bucks that it was Kamone in the picture. The woman's hair, skin color, lips, nose and facial structure were identical to Kamone's. She even had the same eye color and petite figure.

She sat on the edge of the bed and peeled the picture out the album, hoping there was writing on the back that would reveal the woman's identity. Sure enough, written in black ink were the names

Lucci, David and Kathy and in quotation marks by her name was the word "Ma". When Lucci told her she reminded him of his mother she didn't know he was being so literal about it.

Her bladder almost gave way when she heard the music stop and the sound of feet racing up the stairs as David called out her name.

She quickly threw the picture under the covers of the unmade bed before placing the album back against the wall and running over to the dresser as if she had just begun moving it.

"Kamone!" David shouted out from the hall.

"I'm in the bedroom!" she yelled, tussling with the huge dresser.

As David walked into the room, his smile disappeared when he saw Kamone moving the dresser. "What you doing?" he asked defensively, peeking at the photo album from the corner of his eye.

"Oh ... Um, I just started moving this heavy-ass dresser. I thought it would look better in that corner," she pointed. "What you think?" she asked, nervously wiping her wet hands on the sides of the oversized sweats.

"Yeah," he answered, looking at her suspiciously before walking toward the album and bending over to pick it up.

"Oh, I didn't even see that back there," she lied, giving him a fake grin. "What's in there?" she asked reaching out for it, praying he didn't open it.

"It's just some old pictures of a few of my ex

Tanika Lynch

bitches," he replied dryly, smacking it softly against his free hand. "You don't wanna see it."

"Oh ... OK," she replied, breathing sassily as he walked over to the closet and threw it inside.

"What's up wit' you?" he asked, helping her to move the dresser. "You feelin' like Mary Poppins today or what? I see you done cleaned the whole damn house. Is this part of your recovery?" he joked.

"Sorta." She smiled, trying not to make eye contact with him. "I just thought it would make me feel better."

"Yeah," he replied, walking over to her and hugging her from behind. "That OD scared the shit outta me, too. I don't wanna lose you to that China White, Ma. I'm proud of you for leavin' that smack alone."

Kamone's entire body stiffened from his touch. She had an eerie feeling that David felt as though she were actually a reincarnation of his mother.

"Can I get some suga?" he asked, poking out his lips as he turned her around, looking displeased when she gave him a quick peck on the lips.

"What's wrong, Ma? My breath stank or somethin'?" he asked, blowing his breath into his hand.

"No I just ... I um ... I need to take a bath. I look and feel disgusting. I need to soak in some water." She turned to leave.

"I'm comin' with you," he said, walking behind her. "You eva' had that thang sucked under water?"

he smiled.

"Um, I wanna be alone for a while, David," she explained, turning to face him as she stood in the doorway.

"Come on, Ma," he whined, reaching out to grab her hand. He became confused when Kamone jumped at his touch. She had never done that before. "Why you so edgy?" he asked, slightly squeezing her hand.

"Just ... It's just I'm still kinda kicking, and my body is real fidgety, and it's making me cranky," she explained, looking away from him.

"How about while you take your bath, I fry us up some pork chops and pour a few drinks to relax you. Then we can watch some porno flicks, and I can toss yo' salad." He smiled seductively. "You seem to like that."

"I'm not feelin' all that tonight." She smiled, pulling her hand away. "I just wanna relax in the tub and get some sleep. I'm burnt out."

"Oh," he said, rubbing his goatee like Lucci did when deep in thought as he observed her body language. "All right then. I'ma do a few lines before I cook. You still need to eat. You lookin' kinda weak."

"OK," she said, not even bothering to look at him as she walked out the room. She closed the bathroom door and sighed as she pressed her back against it. She knew she had to make her next move fast. David gave her the creeps, and she was scared

Tanika Lynch

to even be around him.

She ran herself a hot bath, playing with the water as she sat nude on the edge of the tub. When she felt the temperature was just right, she got in and sank down in comfort.

She tried to think her plans through, but the woman in the picture kept invading her thoughts. She could hear David's voice calling her Ma, as the writing on the back of the photo played back in her mind.

At first, she just thought it was common slang that David was using. She had heard many men calling women ma, or shortie, but now she felt as though David really meant it. Now she understood why he wanted to steal her from Lucci. It was a psychological thing. He wanted her to love and accept him so badly because he felt his mother never had. It was like she was his second chance.

There was no telling what was rolling around in that sick mind of his, but she knew she had to get away before he endangered her life.

She soaked in the tub for close to an hour, enjoying her relaxation as she thought about Ivory and Paul. Her train of thought was broken when David slowly opened the bathroom door, standing shirtless in a pair of tan boxers and perspiring like he had just finished the Million Man March. His eyes were bloodshot red, and his pupils were extremely dark and glassy. He stared at her with a sinful smirk as he stretched his arms up and rested them

on the wall outside the entrance.

Kamone sat up slowly, giving him an insincere smile as he just stood there, apparently very high.

"Them pork chops sho' smell good," she replied, striking up a conversation to see where his mind was. "I can smell them way up here."

"Um," he huffed, with a slight chuckle. "I guess that dope must still be coming out yo' system cuz you hallucinatin'. I ain't cookin' no pork chops," he replied, walking toward the tub and standing over her with his hand behind his back.

"David, I ..."

"Let's cut out all the bullshit, all right?" he interrupted in a loud, yet calm tone. "What was you snoopin' around for?"

"I wasn't snoopin'. I was just cleanin' up." She leaned away from him.

"You looked at them pictures, Ma?"

Kamone swayed her head back and forth, looking innocent.

"Don't lie to me!" he yelled, stomping his feet like a three-year-old. "I found this under the covers," he said, whipping out the picture he held behind his back. "It didn't just grow legs and walk by itself!"

"OK, OK. I saw them," she answered, developing a lump in her throat.

"What you know about her, huh? What did Lucci tell you?"

"N ... nothing," she stuttered, flinching every

Tanika Lynch

time he made a move.

"He told you, didn't he? I know he told you! That nigga always trying to turn you against me!" he shouted, turning swiftly and punching the mirror on the medicine cabinet, shattering it with one blow.

"It's OK, baby," she said softly, trying to defuse the situation before it got worse.

"You seen him today, didn't you? You met up wit' him today, and you talked about leaving me, didn't you?" he yelled, grabbing his head as if he were hearing voices.

"Baby, no," she whined, becoming fearful. "You're just being paranoid, David. It's the drugs makin' you think like that. I'm not leaving you."

"He's tryin' to take you from me. I can't let him do that. He can't take you from me. You mine this time."

"David, please stop talking like that. I love you and only you. I'm not going anywhere."

"You always loved him more than me," he said in a strange, demonic-sounding voice. "Don't make me do it again, Ma! Don't make me do it!" he grunted, pulling his cheeks down with the palms of his hands as tears shot from his eyes.

"David, I love you. I only love you."

"You lyin'! You don't love me. You think I'm a failure. You said I'd never be shit! You said you hated the day you had me! But I gotta trick for you, Ma. If I can't get no love, neither can Lucci!" before she knew it, he dove into the tub at her and squeezed her neck as he gritted his teeth.

"You made me do it!" he yelled as he strangled Kamone. "You made me, Ma! I thought we could work things out this time, but you still the selfish bitch you always been!"

Kamone gagged, digging her nails into his face, splashing water everywhere as she struggled to get free. She was determined to get away. She wanted to live. She was too young to die! She kneed him in the nuts with all her might, and jumped out as he held himself screaming in pain.

As she tried to run, she slipped and fell in the large puddle of water. She scrambled to get up, but it was too late. David grabbed her ankle and held her there as he climbed out the tub and jumped on her back.

"Gotcha!" he said, slamming her head against the tile several times before grabbing her hair and pulling her to his bedroom.

She cried and screamed, begging for him to stop as he dragged her toward his closet with one hand and grabbed his 12 gauge with the other before dragging her beside his bed and flipping her over onto her back.

"David, please," she cried as he pressed the gun against the left side of her chest. "I'm not your mother! I'm only 15! I love you! I swear to God, I do!"

"All I ever wanted you to do was love me, Ma.

Tanika Lynch

That's all I wanted," he explained through clinched teeth as he lowered the gun to her vagina. "Lucci's your only son, you heartless bitch!" he said, kicking her legs apart and ramming the gauge into her vagina, pushing it farther than her body allowed him to.

Kamone's toes curled as she covered her face and screamed. She was in so much pain that she felt as if she were about to lose consciousness.

"I hate this pussy! I hate the day I came outta it!" he cried, giving her several quick jabs. "It's over, Ma. It's time for you to go back to hell where you came from!" he said, biting his lip as he pulled the trigger.

Kamone lay silent, in shock. Meanwhile, David shook his head as if coming out of a trance. When he heard the gun click, something clicked in his brain, bringing him back to reality. Luckily for her the gun wasn't loaded. He looked down at Kamone who lay shaking in pain, and snatched the gun from inside her. Blood streamed out like an ocean, and big thick clots gushed themselves out.

"I'm sorry!" he cried, dropping the gun to the floor. "I didn't mean to hurt you!"

"Help me," she begged in a weak, straining voice, curling up into the fetal position and moaning in suffering pain.

David stood over her, sobbing hard. He didn't know what to do as he watched the blood continue to fall from her vagina. Kamone let out a loud,

high-pitched squeal when a beige-colored sac fell from her womb.

David became silent, frowning in confusion as he examined the sac. "You was pregnant?" he asked softly, looking back and forth between her and the sac.

Kamone's body shook violently as she held her aching stomach as agonizing pain restrained her from even talking.

"I can't let you leave me." David panicked, knowing that he had done a terrible thing. "I need you! I can't let you leave me!" David snatched a blanket from his bed and threw it over Kamone, placing the sac inside with her. "I'm sorry!" he cried, picking her up and carrying her downstairs, headed toward the basement. "I'm sorry I gotta do this to you, Ma." He sprinted down the basement stairs. "I can't let you leave me! I know you will!" He laid her beside some boxes in the cluttered basement, looking at her sadly as her body still shook. "It's gonna be OK, Ma, but for now I gotta keep you down here for a while. I'll come back to get you when my mind's right, I promise. I know you mad with me right now, but you just don't understand how much I love you." He walked away slowly with his head hung low, turning around to look at her once more before he left. "Sorry 'bout the baby," he said, sounding insincere. "It probably was Lucci's anyways. We gonna have our own babies together. We didn't need that one."

Tanika Lynch

Whore

He hit the light switch and walked up the stairs, locking the door behind him.

Kamone continued to weep as she grabbed hold of the sac that David had placed beside her in the blanket. She placed it to her chest and held it tight, not seeing it as just a sac, but her baby. She let out the most agonizing scream of heartache, torture and misery. She wanted to know why, if there was really a God, he would allow her to suffer so badly in life? Where was this God when she always needed him the most? And if he really loved her, why wouldn't he just take her life instead of allowing her to endure so much anguish?

She lay there in the dark with her dead baby, crying herself to sleep. She knew that tomorrow someone was going to die—even if it was her!

Tanika Lynch

Triple Crown Publications presents . . .

Tanika Lynch

chapter
twenty-one

Lucci sat slouched down in the plushed La-Z-Boy chair in the basement, drinking gin and chain smoking as oldies music played softly on his stereo system. He stared, unamused, at his exotic fish as they swam aimlessly in the built-in aquarium.

He hadn't been the same since Kamone had been gone. Nothing had been the same for that matter. His partners had to handle all his business for him because he couldn't even think straight. They all told him to just forget about her and move on with his life, but he couldn't. When she left, a piece of him went along with her, and without her, he was only half the man he used to be.

He couldn't eat, sleep and even began to question his judgment. He didn't know if he had made the right decision by putting her out in the streets like that after having knowledge of all the horrible things she had been through. He knew he had reacted with his heart and not with his head. Now

he was heartbroken and regretted ever flying out to California.

Ivory and Paul wouldn't even speak to him, let alone come near him after witnessing him beat Kamone the way he did. They weren't active like they once were, and the only time they ate was when Ivory snuck them food in the middle of the night when she thought he was asleep.

He turned up his bottle of gin wondering where Kamone was right now? If she was hungry? Hurt? Or more importantly, still alive? He hated himself for what he had done and he couldn't shake the thought that she really might be out there in the street, pregnant with his child. He realized that regardless of what he saw on that videotape, he coulda dealt with the situation like a man. Now it was too late. The streets probably had her lost and turned out to the point of no return.

As he sat there, a song by Luther Ingram entitled "If Loving You is Wrong," ripped through his speakers and he couldn't help but to cry as he reminisced. It was their favorite song and they would sing it to each other periodically throughout the day. He blasted his stereo to capacity and sang along as memories of Kamone's beautiful voice soared through his imagination.

He had his eyes closed, singing with all his heart when he felt a light tap on his arm. He jumped, turning toward the touch and looked dead into the watery eyes of Ivory as she stood beside

Tanika Lynch

the chair holding her original Barbie doll that had once belonged to Kamone.

He sat up straight and used his remote to turn down the music to hear what Ivory had to say.

"Is sister home now?" she questioned in a moaning voice, poking out her shivering lip as she heaved close to crying.

Lucci lowered his head in guilt and sorrow, realizing that Ivory recognized that this certain song was Kamone's favorite, and as it hadn't been played since Kamone had been gone, Ivory thought she was home when she heard it.

"Can we talk for a minute, piggy baby?" Lucci asked, kindly looking at her with soft eyes.

Ivory stared at him hesitantly for a moment before shaking her head slowly in agreement and climbing onto his lap where he patted for her to sit.

"Piggy baby." He looked at the child as she played with her doll. "I'm sorry for what I did to Kamone. And I'm really sorry that you and Paul saw it. What I did was dumb. I acted really stupid."

"Yeah," she agreed, bouncing her head up and down. "You was a big stupid head."

"I know," he replied holding back a smile, wanting to laugh at Ivory's comment. "But Kamone has a problem, and she's been trying to deal with that problem for a long time. And I overreacted because she lied to me and told me her problem was gone."

"What kinda problem?" she asked, still stroking her doll's burnt hair.

237

"The kinda problem that's too complicated for a seven-year-old to understand."

"Do you love sister?"

"I love her with all my heart. Probably more than I love myself."

"If you love sister you wouldn't be mad at her because her got a problem. You suppose to help her with her problems." Ivory looked up into his face and replied, "Sister told me when people love each other they stay together for eber and eber. Her said no matter what happens they stick together like me, her and Paul. We'll always love each other no matter what."

Lucci took a deep breath, feeling ashamed by the fact that a small child knew more about real love than he did.

"I miss sister," she whined, laying her head against his chest.

"I do, too," he replied, rubbing Ivory's back. "I miss her smile and the way she laughed. I miss everything about her."

"I miss her playing hide and seek with me and Paul." Ivory giggled. "'Member that time you and sister was playing the flour game?"

"What flour game?" he asked, not remembering playing such a game.

"You know, the one when sister had all the flour on her face like a clown and you had Paul's play gun pointing at her and when I came in the house you tried to hide it, cuz you didn't want me to

Tanika Lynch

know you a big man who still plays with toys." She giggled, looking up at him.

"When was this, piggy baby?" he asked, looking puzzled.

"You know, the day sister tricked me, and said you was in another state, but you wasn't. You was sittin' on the couch next to sister, and ya'll lady friend. Her was pretty," Ivory explained nonchalantly, moving the arms of her doll.

"Did I say anything to you?" he asked, wondering if she was talking about a dream that had seemed real to her.

"Um huh. You called me a trick baby, 'member? And I said my name not trick baby it's piggy baby. And then you told me I had pretty hair and pretty eyes like you hadn't even remembered me," she said, batting her lashes.

"Was sister crying or anything when she had the flour on her face?"

"No, but her got mad at me, and pushed me." She frowned, remembering the incident. "Her told me to go outside, and not come back 'til her get us. We was outside all day, and when her came and got us, her was lookin' drunk, and her was crying then."

Lucci's heart weighed heavy in his chest as Ivory told her story. He knew immediately that Ivory had mistaken him for David, as she was unaware that he had a twin.

"Oh, and ..." Ivory cut her sentence short, look-

ing down at her doll, as if she were afraid to speak.

"What is it Ivory? You can say it," he said, sensing her fear.

"You not gonna get mad at me?" she asked, biting her small finger.

"I'd never get mad at you, baby. You can tell me anything."

"When sister told us to stay outside, I had to pee-pee real bad. I tried to hold it, but it was hurting. So I snuck in the house, and you was making sister do bad things to the pretty lady down there," she said, pointing to her privates. "And you put them on the TV thing. Sister was crying then, too. Don't you 'member?" she said, tilting her head and looking at him as if he were well aware of what she was talking about. "I was so scared, I just went back outside and peed in the grass."

Lucci's heart almost stopped, and the room began to spin around him as he realized the truth of what happened while he was away in California. That dirty bastard David had struck again, and Lucci felt like a fool for allowing David to turn him against Kamone.

He jolted up the stairs with Ivory to prepare to go out and find the woman he loved. And he had a pretty good first guess as to where she might be!

Tanika Lynch

chapter
twenty-two

David picked lint off his white shirt as he stood in the mirror that was connected to his dresser. He leaned in closer and examined the deep ugly gashes that Kamone had scratched into his face. He had already concocted a story to explain the marks if anyone should inquire about them.

He slapped his baseball cap onto his head and straightened his belt buckle before grabbing his keys and heading downstairs to the kitchen.

He grabbed a large bag of Doritos out the cabinet before opening the refrigerator and picking up an open bag of thinly-sliced ham and a full container of Sunny Delight.

He placed the items under his arm and slowly opened the basement door. He stood at the top of the stairs squinting as he looked around the dimly-lit room for Kamone. "I brought you somethin' to eat," he said, throwing the food down the stairs and watching as it tumbled to the dirty cement

floor. "I ... I thought you might be hungry. It should hold you over until I get back." He took a deep breath, placing his hands on his hips before saying, "I know you might need a bath and I wanna let you outta here, but I think you might try to get away from me, Ma, and I can't let that happen. Now if you promise me that you'll be cool I'll let you take a bath tonight."

He stood there in silence waiting for a response but only heard the noises that the old house made. "I'm going to make a few runs now. I'll be back in a few hours to check on you before I go to work." He turned to close the door but a thought hit him, and he turned back around. "I know you might be still mad at me and I ... I'm sorry about last night. I don't know what came over me. I didn't mean to hurt you like that. I truly do love you and you'll learn to love me, too." He shook his head in shame at himself as he softly closed the door, locking it behind him.

Kamone held her breath as she listened to his footsteps walking around upstairs. She could hear the squeaky noise of the alarm system then the sound of the front door slamming. She waited until she heard his engine start up before standing to her unsteady feet, tottering her way across the room and began rummaging through the litter that furnished the basement.

Kamone knew that David would probably be back sooner than he lead her to believe and she

Tanika Lynch

planned to be long gone before that time ever came. She wasn't about to risk trying to escape while he was there or whenever he allowed her out the basement. For all she knew, he was still in the sick phase of believing that she was his mother and she wasn't about to wait around for a death that was sure to come.

She picked up everything she thought could break down the door or pop the lock, but nothing seemed to work. She cried out in anger, losing all hope as she threw the useless instruments to the floor.

She screamed in disappointment as she knocked a crowd of boxes around, releasing her built-up fury and to her surprise, when she knocked over one particular box, an abundance of tools came crashing to the ground.

She fell to her knees, looking as if she had struck gold and she picked up a small screwdriver and a mallet. Her chest tightened in anxiety as she crawled with weakened knees up the dirty, wooden stairs. She jammed the slender tip of the screwdriver into the keyhole of the cheap brass doorknob and with every muscle in her tired body, she swung the mallet and hit the screwdriver in deeper with hopes of popping the lock.

When the door flew open, the summer sun shined in her face. She let out an exhausted jittery giggle as she allowed the mallet to slip from her hand. She quickly got over the initial shock of

being free as she darted to the door like a runaway slave, realizing she wasn't totally free yet.

She flung back the front door and grabbed the armor gate to open it and get out, but it was locked and she didn't know where he hid his spare keys.

She began rattling it, screaming for help as several neighbors across the street sat on their porches enjoying the summer air. But everyone just looked at the naked, bloody girl like she was crazy. They knew whose house she was in and no one would dare step foot on deranged David's property, not even with permission.

She cried frantically as she began searching around the house for a key—any key. She knew that the entire house was secured with gates, even the windows, and if she didn't get out now David would surely kill her when he got back and saw what she had done.

She ran upstairs into his bedroom, remembering seeing a few keys lying around. She tore the room apart in less than seconds in search for the key. When she went into his closet, she pulled down a box that sat on his top shelf. She didn't find a key, but she did find a loaded .357 Magnum and she knew it might come in handy if David came back before she could get away.

She began tossing his clothes onto the floor after patting them and by luck she patted down his winter police coat and the sound of keys jingling teased her ear. She dug into the pockets and found

Tanika Lynch

a metal key ring that held several different sets of keys.

She threw on one of his T-shirts to cover her nakedness and headed down the hall on her way back to the front door. But before she could make it to the steps, she heard the sound of David's voice calling her from a distance, yet close by. The sound of his blaring voice intimidated her to the point that she began to urinate onto David's black carpet as she stood panicking, undecided as to what she should do. A small voice in her head told her to run and hide. She quickly turned on her heels and crept back into the bedroom, gliding under the bed.

She shook as if she were lying on ice, listening to his thunderous voice calling for her as he searched the house. What she didn't realize was that the voice wasn't calling out to her in anger but grief. It was Lucci who had parked his car around the block and used the keys that David once gave him to get into the back door.

He knew for certain that David wasn't home. He had called David earlier that morning as if everything were back to normal and arranged for David to make a dry run that would take him a good while to figure out, leaving more than enough time for him to search the house for Kamone, and he wasn't leaving without her!

Thinking that she might be hiding from him in fear, Lucci called out to her. He explained that he

wasn't mad with her anymore. He was unaware of what had taken place between her and David, and his plea only sounded like David trying to con her into coming out.

She gripped the gun firmly, placing her finger on the trigger as she heard him making his way up the stairs. Her mouth became dry as she prepared herself for what she was about to do. She had no choice but to kill him just as soon as he got within eye range. She knew that if she didn't, he would torture her to a slow death.

The neighbors sat on their porches, watching in excitement as David pulled up into his driveway, wondering what he would do to the bloody naked girl who he was obviously holding captive in his home. He paid no attention to their smirks and stares as he walked onto the porch, dialing numbers on his cellular.

He had absentmindedly forgotten the drugs that Lucci had sent him to take to J-Smooth, and had been trying to contact Lucci to let him know that he would be running late, but Lucci wasn't answering his cellular, or his home phone.

His killer instincts quickly kicked in when he walked onto his porch and noticed that his front door was wide open, and his belongings had been thrown around. He dropped his phone and jumped to the side, spontaneously pulling his gun. He looked around his neighborhood, realizing that his neighbors knew something as they all looked

Tanika Lynch

away, not wanting to be a witness to whatever he had going on.

He quietly keyed open the gate, holding his gun aimed straight forward, as he stepped inside, observing the mess. His first thought was that Kamone had somehow gotten free, and was looking for away out until he heard Lucci's voice calling out her name upstairs.

Kamone inhaled as her trembling hand extended, pointing the gun straight as she watched Lucci get on one knee, about to lift the blanket that draped the sides of the bed so that he could get a better view.

"What the fuck you doin', nigga?" David questioned, speaking through clenched teeth as he placed his Glock handgun to the back of Lucci's head, stopping him from looking under the bed.

Lucci held his hands up in the air, caught off guard. "Where is she?" he asked, standing to his feet. "All I want is my woman and I'll leave, dog. Ain't no need for this shit. We brothas."

"Yo' woman?" David chuckled, allowing Lucci to turn around and face him. "Nigga, she my bitch now. Remember? You didn't want the bitch cuz you seen her eatin' a lil' ass. You done snuck yo' ass up in my crib and shit, you slick-ass chump. You planned this shit, didn't you? You know I got all rights to legally ice yo' ass."

"David, I'm yo' brotha," Lucci said as beads of sweat began to form on his forehead. "Yo' own

flesh and blood. I'm the only mutha fucka who been there for you after what you did. And you gone kill me, after you was the one in the wrong?"

"You damn right." David frowned. "I don't give a fuck 'bout no flesh and blood nigga. David Valentine ain't neva' had nobody but his damn self. I heard what you told that broad. You don't give a fuck 'bout me. You call yo' self usin' me for my services. That shit kinda hurt my feelins, but I hit you where it hurt too, didn't I? I took that lil' bitch you was lovin' so tough, turned her back out on dope, made her lick some twat and you best believe I tore her pussy out the frame every night. I see why you was all in love." He laughed, knowing he was getting under Lucci's skin. "Oh, yeah, I got rid of her problem, too. I meant to send you my condolences."

"What problem?" Lucci frowned, already steaming in anger.

"That ugly-ass baby of yours she was carrying. Too bad you wasn't here to see the delivery. It came out lookin' just like yo' punk ass. A sac of soft mushy shit." He chuckled, holding his stomach in laughter.

Lucci bit his bottom lip so hard that he drew his own blood trying to restrain himself from doing something stupid that would get him killed. David had not only destroyed his relationship but had taken the life of his unborn child. He wanted so badly to grab the gun that was in the backside

Tanika Lynch

of his waist and blow him away. But David had the upper hand and if he didn't think of a way to disarm him fast, he was as good as dead.

"Just tell me one thang, man," Lucci said, biding his time. "What'd I ever do to you? How could you not have a conscience when it comes to your own family?"

"Family?" David yelled, mean-mugging Lucci. "What muthafuckin' family did I have? Everybody was to busy kissin' yo' ass for being on the honor roll and all that nerdy shit! I was a outcast cuz you always wanted to out-do me! You wanna know what you did to me?" he shouted with globs of saliva squirting from his mouth like a rabies-infected dog. "You destroyed my life! And I killed Ma to destroy you! It's yo' fault she dead!"

"I'm sorry you felt that way," Lucci replied unsympathetically.

"Sorry?" he said, biting his lip as he twisted the gun into position on Lucci's forehead. "Sorry don't change shit, nigga! Sorry can't give Ma back her life! Sorry can't erase what I went through in that boys' home! You don't know what them niggaz did to me every night for what I did! Say yo' prayers and hope you get into heaven, you sorry-ass bitch!"

"Wait!" Lucci plead, seeing the look of death in David's eyes. "If you gonna take my life ... do it like a man and not like the bitch they made you in jail! Whoop my ass and take my life, bitch!" Lucci

challenged.

A corrupt smirk crossed David's lips as he looked at Lucci as if he were the one who had gone insane.

"You think you can take me?" he roared, pushing his pistol deeper into Lucci's skull. "I'll snap yo'neck! I'm a man! A grown-ass man!" he hollered, beating his chest like a gorilla with his free hand.

"Prove it, bitch," Lucci smirked, seeing his words had affected David's ego like he hoped they would.

Before Lucci could blink good, David threw his gun onto the bed and uppercut him so hard that he immediately lost his wind. Lucci didn't have time to even think about what had just happened, David hit him again knocking him to the floor. As David went to grab his gun, Lucci noticed Kamone's small feet curled up under the bed. He quickly regained his composure, grabbing David's ankles, bringing him down with a thump on his back and knocking the gun out of his grasp. Both men jumped up at once, going blow for blow. Fighting like strangers in the streets.

Kamone's heart banged, breaking her out into a cold sweat as she listened to the two fighting. Her mouth was as dry as cotton as she lay there in shock, honestly afraid to death. She knew she had to do something. Lucci was out there fighting for her, ready to die for her as she lay under the bed like a coward with a gun. She took a deep breath as she rolled from under the bed, aiming the gun, ready to help her man. But when she looked at the two, who were locked up like battling bulls and both dressed in white, she was unable to tell them apart. She jumped to her feet waving the gun back and forth as they tussled to get free from each other.

Lucci noticed her out the corner of his eye looking faint-hearted and pale and she shifted the gun back and forth in confusion. Even in the serious situation he was in, he didn't want to put her through anything more than he already had. He rejected the thought of allowing her to have David's blood on her hands. This fight was his, and he would never intentionally put her in harm's way.

"Baby, run!" he yelled, trying his best to reach for his gun as David hindered him.

Kamone looked on in horror as she inched toward the door. She began to cry like she had never ever cried before, then she ran for the door. Hesitating, she stopped when she got to the unlocked gate, looking back toward the stairs, hoping to God that Lucci made it out. In that split second, she made a drastic decision. Her life flashed like lighting before her eyes, and all her hardships weighed heavily on her heart. She ran from the house sobbing, knowing that Paul and Ivory would now really be on their own. She couldn't take it

anymore. She wanted to go home, and no one could stop her.

Lucci and David continued to fight all over the room, breaking everything in their path from the bed to the bedroom window, drawing one another's blood in their passionate combative scuffle.

David had more strength, but Lucci had speed and martial arts skills. Lucci was getting the best of David, until he tripped over a lamp that had fallen to the floor, and fell onto his back. David saw his opportunity to finish Lucci off, and took it. He lunged onto Lucci, keeping Lucci down with his body weight and punching him in the face ceaselessly until Lucci became disoriented and lacked in strength.

"Who's the bitch now?" David yelled, standing to his feet and kicking him in the stomach.

"Don't nevah disrespect a grown man!" he proclaimed, struggling for breath as he unzipped his pants. "I dreamed of the day I would do this to you," he said, holding his member in his hand and spraying urine all over Lucci's defenseless body, snickering all the while. "After I kill you, I think I'll take over yo' life." He zipped up his pants. "Drive all yo' cars, spend all yo' money and I might even take yo' name." He bent down over Lucci's face. "I can't wait to move into my new house and sit butt-naked on that soft mink couch. Oh, wait. I already did, when I was bangin' yo' bitch." He hulked up snot and spit it into Lucci's

Tanika Lynch

face. "Her pussy was almost as good as Ma's." He let out a maniacal laugh. "When you get to hell, make sho' you tell her how much I miss her." He stood up, looking around the room for his gun. He turned his back to Lucci when he spotted it lying on the floor by the broken dresser.

David's words sank deeply into Lucci's head, and images of the disgraceful way he had left their mother drifted through his mind. He saw the strife in Kamone's saddened eyes on that tape David had made, and heard the mourning wails of Paul and Ivory as he beat Kamone over David's lies, before tossing her into the streets to undergo more suffering. His heart could feel the pain that David had caused them all, and it gave him a boost of needed energy. He couldn't allow David to hurt another innocent person ever again in this lifetime, and he felt the need to seek revenge for not only himself, but for the hundreds of people David had hurt throughout his life.

He quietly reached for his gun as David walked over to retrieve his own gun. "David!" he yelled, sitting up and closing one eye as he aimed.

David whipped around in surprise, and caught a bullet in his thick chest. He covered his wound with his hands, appearing stunned as Lucci pulled the trigger again, hitting him in both legs and dropping him to his knees.

Lucci stood up sluggishly, wiping blood from his nose as he stared at David. "I shoulda did this

years ago," he said, holding David at gunpoint as he moved in closer.

"I didn't know you had the balls," David chuckled as bubbles of blood began to spout from his mouth. "I guess you think you gonna kill ice now, huh? You wanna be the hero who killed the notorious David Valentine," he said, dropping his hand from his wound, wheezing for air as he reached down and picked up a long, sharp piece of broken glass. "You shot me, but I can't let you kill me," he laughed, gripping the glass so tight that it sliced through his hand.

"What? You gonna kill me with that?" Lucci asked sarcastically.

"David Valentine is too much man to go out like a punk," he smirked. "I can't wait to go to hell and pinch yo' mama's soft ass. But before I let a lil' pussy like you take me out the game, I'll take myself out." He raised his arms to plunge the glass into his heart, but before he could, Lucci shot his hands and shattered the glass to pieces.

"This for Mama!" he cried. He lowered his gun and shot David's penis. "And this for Ma and the world!" he yelled, shooting him several times in his chest and stomach.

David swayed back and forth on his knees, refusing to fall as his thick, dark blood covered his bedroom floor. His eyes rolled around in his head as he gave Lucci a weak grin, sticking up his middle finger.

Tanika Lynch

Whore

"Fuck you, too," Lucci smirked, emptying the rest of his clip into David's head. Pieces of his face and brain matter splattered the walls as he fell backwards in an awkward position. Lucci continued to pull the trigger of the empty gun, wishing he had more bullets to put into his body. When he realized what he was doing, he threw the gun at David and spit at him before turning around mercilessly and staggering out the room.

All the neighbors had heard the shots and came out of their homes, gathering around watching and whispering, wondering what the outcome would be. When they saw Lucci tottering from the house bloody and badly beaten, they became rowdy and made lewd remarks, thinking he was David.

"They shoulda killed cha', muthafucka!" the old lady next door yelled before turning around on her walker to shamble back into her house.

The crowd slowly began to disperse.

"I ... I'm not David, I'm his brother! David's dead," he explained to the crowd as he stood in the middle of them, holding his head and looking around frantically. "My girl! Where's my girl!" he hollered.

"Yo, dog," a young man said, walking up to Lucci. "I seen her walking down the street with a gun in her hand. She bent that corner," he explained, pointing to the area. "Me and my cousins wanted to help her cuz she was bleeding. But we thought she might cap us, cuz she was

looking all bugged out and shit."

Lucci could hear people talking about David being dead as he slowly jogged passed them, headed to the corner. He picked up his pace when he noticed specks of blood on the concrete leading a pathway to wherever she was. "Kamone!" he screamed, running full speed, following the blood.

Tears dripped from Kamone's face as she stood in front of the church, a vacant look in her eyes. She could hear the husky voice of the woman who sang inside as the members of the church shouted in worship. She climbed the stairs in a dreamlike mental state, swinging the doors wide open and walking inside on steady feet.

People began to scream in horror while others ran from the church in terror. The choir stopped singing, stuck in shock as the elders of the church sat open-mouthed and holding their chests as she made her way to the alter looking like a walking corpse with blood still leaking and drying up on her feet and legs.

"My God," Mr. Roberts said, softly rising to his feet from his cushioned chair in the pulpit as the preacher backed away, thinking she had come to hurt someone.

Kamone fell to her weary knees as Mr. Roberts slowly approached, wearing his Deacon's robe.

"I'm tired," she said in a whisper as Mr. Roberts stood near by, not wanting to frighten her while she held the gun. "I can't take it anymore, Mr.

Tanika Lynch

Roberts."

Tears began to well up in Mr. Roberts' eyes as he looked down at Kamone, already seeing everything she had experienced. "The Lord told me you was coming," he said as his tears began to fall. "I've been waiting for you, chile. God has been watchin' over you."

Kamone held the gun tightly as tears flowed down her face onto her neck, wetting the front of her T-shirt. "Why me? If God loves me so much why would he do this to me?" she questioned, looking into Mr. Roberts' soft eyes. "If He's been watchin' over me, why have I been hurt and abused so much? I neva did nothing wrong to nobody! Why do I deserve this terrible life?"

Members of the church began to cry out for the girl, calling on the Lord and speaking in tongues as they held hands, praying for this child who was ready to take her own life which was so short-lived.

"Chile," Mr. Roberts cried. "Don't you realize what the Lord has in store for you? He has a strong callin' on yo' life, and what you've been through was only necessary. You are a leader of people. God has anointed you to show others the way to salvation. You had to feel their heartache to relate from the heart. How can you show them how to get through the rain and see the sunshine, unless you been there?

"God's been waiting for you to come to him so

he can end your cycle of despair. And I speak it in the name of Jesus that it ends right here, right now!" he shouted, lifting his hands upward as if receiving divine power from the Heavens. "Trust in yo' Lord and savior! He says you won't leave this earth 'til He finished wit' cha, and honey, He ain't even got started!" The members began to form a circle around Kamone, praying to themselves as Mr. Roberts continued to preach. Everyone could feel the presence of God. There was no doubt that he was among them, surrounding Kamone in his love.

"I wanna die," she wept, gripping the gun even tighter. "I wanna go to that place you called paradise. You told me there's no suffering up there. No more crying ... no more pain."

"But yo' Heavenly Father isn't ready for you yet. You got so much to look forward to, and you just don't know it yet. There's a reason and a season for everything and everyone. Our small human minds can't even begin to think like God. Your life has purpose and God made you stronger than some other folk cuz what he put you here to do is very important. If you take your own life, you'll neva' see all the wonderful gifts he has in store for you."

At that moment, Lucci burst through the door and saw Kamone on her knees with the gun at her side as the believers encircled her. "Kamooone!" he cried, running toward her as she placed the gun

Tanika Lynch

to her head. He felt as if he couldn't get there fast enough, just like the day his mother died.

"If what you say is true, God won't let me die," she whimpered. "I'm sorry," she sobbed, closing her eyes. "I hope He forgives me."

"Nooo!" Mr. Roberts hollered as he miraculously threw his aging body at Kamone, knocking the gun from her hand but not before it fired.

The blast from the gun had deafened her ears to all sound. Slowly, Kamone opened her eyes, people were all around her. She could see their mouths moving but had no clue as to what was going on. Mr. Roberts stayed by her side while other church members rushed over to help the person who'd been struck by the stray bullet. Over her shoulder Kamone could see Lucci's body sprawled out. *My God, what did I do?* she asked herself, realizing that the bullet missed her and hit Lucci. Kamone rolled onto her knees and crawled over to Lucci.

The bullet had ripped through his left shoulder, and he was bleeding profusely. Lucci's face was creased with pain. Some of his pain began to cease when he saw Kamone leaning over him holding his right hand. Lucci told her, "I'm so sorry, I love you."

Still unable to hear, Kamone tried desperately to read his lips through her teary eyes. The only words that she could make out were *love you.* "I love you, too," Kamone sobbed. Suddenly she was

pulled away from Lucci by two female paramedics, while three male paramedics began working on him. As she was wheeled toward the ambu-
lance, Kamone looked to the sky with an oxygen
mask covering her face and she said to God, "You
didn't let me die. I guess you do love me, huh? I
give in Lord, I submit to your ways. Just please
make a change in me. Tell the devil he can't have
me. I'm yours."

Tanika Lynch

epilogue

"Sometimes things don't go as we feel they should." Kamone paused and stared at the young girls before her. It had been a year and three months since she'd attempted suicide. After vigorous psychiatric treatment, her life had become somewhat stable and she spent her days giving speeches at high schools and juvenile detention centers. The lifeless looks in the young girls' eyes at this particular all-female detention center had compelled Kamone to give up her entire story. She'd given it to them raw and uncensored. All of the girls sat attentive and focused after hearing the horrific nightmare that Kamone once called her life. Now their eyes were burning with fire. Her struggle and survival showed them that they, too, could overcome their circumstances.

A few of the girls sat on the edge of their chairs with tears rolling down their cheeks listening intently as Kamone wrapped up her speech. "In

life, people have a choice as to whether their lives will have a happy ending or not. But what most don't realize is their lives do not belong to them. All of our lives belong to God we are here for his purpose and his purpose only. I tried to end mine the way I wanted to without realizing God had a greater plan for me. Had I taken my own life, which I felt at the time was the only way out, I would've never gotten the chance to give Paul and Ivory my strong love and support that they'll need to grow up and become successful. I would've never known the joy of making Lucci a happy man on our wedding day. I would've missed out on the pleasure of raising our twin sons that are growing in my womb. If my suicide had been successful, my entire life would have been in vain and a great disappointment to my heavenly Father because ... because I would never have encountered young ladies like you—the abused and troubled children whose lives hopefully will be changed and inspired by my life story. Now, because I am here before you a living testimony of love, hope, and faith, you too can see that the cycle of despair in your lives can be broken!"

Tanika Lynch

Whore

Tanika Lynch